Christmas in Side Lake

THE TURTLE CREEK SERIES
BOOK FOUR

JENNIFER WALTERS

BARBRA JUNE PUBLISHING

Christmas in Side Lake

The Turtle Creek Series
Book 4

By Jennifer Walters

For my mother
AKA Mother Christmas

Thank you for always making
Christmas so magical,
and always having the best
Christmas lights in town.

Other books by Jennifer Walters

The Turtle Creek Series

The Memories We Keep

A Side Lake Summer

Return to Side Lake

Christmas in Side Lake

The Fredrickson's Series

Always Right Here

Northern Winds

Greenrock Road

Standalone

The Weight of Change

www.JenniferWaltersAuthor.com

Brief Character overview from the Series

Maddy +
    Brad+
    Tim_____
    Love Triangle

Lyndsey+(Brad's sister)
    Kevin +
    Tracey_____
    Love Triangle

Kat+
    Ethan +
    Andy_____
    Love Triangle

Lizzy+ (Victoria's Niece)
    Tim +
    Dalton_____
    Love Triangle

Whitney + Josh = Daughter **Brittany**
    Victoria + Troy (Kevin's Brother)= **Hope**

Chapter One

Lizzy

AROUND NOON, he turned off the television. His footsteps creaked behind me, which made my heart race. He was always right on time, not a minute early or late. But I was ready for him. I had finished three loads of laundry and folded and put everything away. The floor was mopped, the shelves dusted, and I had ham and cheese sandwiches on the table, cut diagonally just the way he liked.

He nodded in approval as he stared at the plates of food, his hand reaching around my back to pull me in. His lips pressed against mine, the smell of his breath rancid. He reached his hand down my back and stopped as he grabbed my butt, squeezing it so hard I flinched.

I squealed and let out a laugh to make him think I was enjoying it as he made his way inside my waistband and squeezed my bottom again.

Maybe food would stop the pawing. "Hungry?"

He nodded and sat down at the small glass table. The table was a bit unsteady, the glass just resting on the stand. Dalton brought it home one day, but I figured he probably stole it or picked it up at the junk-yard. A place to eat was a nice change since all we had for furniture was an old couch, Dalton's gaming chair, and a giant television and desk for his computer system.

He took a bite from his sandwich and glanced at me. "What time do you have to work?"

"One o'clock. Do you think you could give me a ride, or should I just take the car?"

He stared at me for an uncomfortable minute as he chewed on his sandwich. His eyes never left my face. He swallowed. "I'll drop you off," he said with a warning in his voice. "But you'll come with me to run an errand on the way."

My lungs deflated at the thought. When Dalton and I first dated, I thought the way he loved to take risks was sexy, and he was never afraid to stand up for me when my shy demeanor caused others to walk all over me. But I soon realized when my friends stopped returning my calls and Dalton was rude to their boyfriends that he was never my hero. He was just a jerk.

And a drug dealer, but that just added to the bad boy routine I fell in love with. Now it was the way we paid our bills, and I did not stop him. He would never listen anyway.

He was smart about his drug trade. He told no one where we lived, and he hid the drug baggies in the closet of our small one bedroom duplex, but it still made me nervous. Dalton told me I was worrying too much, and I knew without him we would probably starve. He was too smart to ever get caught

We finished our sandwiches, and I changed into my scrubs before meeting him in the car. Dalton was not a fan of waiting, and he liked me without makeup, which made it much easier to get ready.

"Can you find a ride home tonight? I'd rather not worry about stopping my game just to pick you up." His eyes stared ahead at the road. He never noticed when I did not reply. And he really didn't care what I had to say anyway.

I hated asking my co-workers for a ride home, and he knew it. None of them lived near me, and I hated to be a burden. But Dalton gave me no choice. I'd stopped having an opinion or a voice long ago and sometimes it felt like a blessing not to have to talk. Not to have to think at all. He handled everything.

Dalton pulled the car into the bumpy alley and slid into a spot behind a one-stall garage with yellow paint peeling off the siding and broken windows.

"I'll wait here," I said as I looked down at my hands. I knew better than to look him straight in the eyes, or he would say I was trying to challenge him.

Luckily, he didn't look at me at all. He grabbed the paper bag and disappeared around the garage. I jumped when he came back a minute or two later, only he was not alone. Two guys followed close behind him. Dalton walked to the car with hunched shoulders, his face sweaty and pale.

I knew the moment I saw him, my instincts were right on. Something was off. Something did not feel right. Dalton never brought people back to the car or hung out with them outside the deals. The hairs on the back of my neck stood on end, and a shiver shot down my spine. We were in trouble.

He looked so vulnerable as he approached the driver's door.

The back doors opened and slammed shut. Something told me not to turn around and look at the men. Cold, hard metal pushed against the back of my head and I froze. The other guy had a gun pointed at Dalton's side.

"Just drive," a deep voice from behind us said.

What the hell did Dalton get us into? We might get shot and on top of that, I was going to be late for work and get fired.

These criminals were going to find out where we lived. Would they even let us live once they got what they wanted?

"What do they want?" I whispered.

"Shut your mouth, you dumb bitch, or I'll put a bullet in your big mouth. Drive!" the man demanded.

The guy leaned toward me and put his mouth next to my ear. "Give me your phone and your purse," he whispered in a malicious tone, taunting me.

His breath made me gag. I handed my phone to him over my shoulder.

Dalton pushed on the pedal, and the tires squealed. If he got pulled over, we would either be shot or the cops would see the guns and we would all end up in jail. What would I tell the officer? That we were dealing drugs, and they robbed us at gunpoint to steal our illegal drugs? These thugs knew they'd never get caught because we would be in too much trouble if we were to rat on them.

Though only minutes, it felt like hours had gone by when we finally reached our house. I just wanted that feeling of metal on my skin to go away.

A part of me was hoping Dalton had a plan, and he would not take these criminals into our home. Then again, they had my phone and my wallet with my ID. I never updated my new address so the thug would only know where my grandparents lived, but that was probably worse.

If he refused to take the thugs into our house, we would probably end up shot. Dalton had no choice. These guys were terrifying, and I doubted we were their first victims. We could always move and change our identities, if we came out of this alive.

"Don't move a damn inch until I tell you to." He paused and all I could hear was the sound of my own loud breathing. "Now, pull out your keys, slowly, and we'll follow you to the house. Don't do anything stupid."

I opened my door and the creepy guy with the gun snuck out right behind me. He pushed the gun up under my jacket and into my side.

"You best not try anything," he whispered into my ear.

The cruel sound of his voice made my stomach curdle, and my hands shake.

Once inside, the other guy followed Dalton to the space in the closet where he stored his drugs. Hundreds of dollars in marijuana was now gone. There went all Dalton's play money. And now Dalton would want my paycheck so we would once again be behind on our rent and probably end up evicted.

But at least I'd still be alive.

Dalton gave him my backpack and put the baggies in it.

"It was nice doing business with you," the guy said, inches from Dalton's face to taunt and intimidate him. He did not break eye contact, and Dalton did not look away either. The guy spit in his face and Dalton still did not move.

Please leave. Please leave.

The guy that had yet to leave my side or give me an inch of space said, "Why don't the two of you give us a ride home now?"

Are you kidding me?

I did not want to sit in the car with them again. With a loaded gun held to my side or my head. Was it loaded? I wasn't sure I wanted to know the answer to that.

There had to be another way. But there wasn't, and before I knew it, we were back in the car. I wanted to cry, scream, or, if I was brave enough, run away.

My mind buzzed as we drove through the streets. This situation was not fair and riding in the car with the nasty dealers was torture. If they even thought for a second Dalton would be back to sell them pot again, they were wrong. This was wrong.

The guns were no longer pushing against us as we drove down the highway, but it did not make me feel any better. They were laughing and joking behind us. One of them opened a back window.

We pulled up in front of their house, and one guy leaned into the front seat between us. "I hope you have insurance on your phones." He laughed and slapped the head rest behind Dalton's seat. We both jumped.

Our phones were gone. He threw them out the window, but at least we were going to live.

The jangle of keys and other stuff dropped to the floor in the back seat. My purse. He was dumping everything from my purse on the floor in the back seat.

"You two have a wonderful day now." With a smirk, he held up both our ID's in an effort to intimidate us. It worked.

For the first time, I turned my head and looked at him. I would show no fear. Three missing teeth, pronounced cheekbones, and sunken eyes stared back at me.

The minute he shut the door, I broke down with relief, knowing I was going to live. I covered my eyes. My body trembled, weak and exhausted from the altercation.

Dalton never even looked my way or asked if I was okay. He drove past the road to take me to work. Did he forget, or was this his way of telling me he was not letting me go to work?

My body was paralyzed at the thought of returning home.

My hands shook, and I was dizzy.

I had to ask him. There was a chance he just forgot or thought I would not want to go to work. "Dalton, I need to get to work."

He pulled a flip phone out of his pocket and threw it in my lap.

"Call them," he ordered.

"Where did you get this phone?" When did he start carrying a second phone? Why would he even have a second phone?

His face reddened, and his hands clenched the steering wheel. "Just call, damn it, Lizzy! Pick up the phone and call. It's not that difficult."

"But...but we need the money. All your weed is gone, and we can't afford for me to miss this shift."

He turned and glared at me. My body trembled.

"Fine," he growled through clenched teeth.

He turned the car around in the middle of the highway and drove across the ditch in the median. I held on tight and squeezed my eyes shut, waiting for the Blazer to roll, but it somehow stayed upright as the wheels bounced around in the soft grass. Cars honked as we drove back onto the road. One lady even gave us the finger, but Dalton did not seem to notice.

I was sure he was trying to kill us. Angry at the world for what ultimately was his own fault. I wanted to get out of our vehicle and run as far and fast as I could, and never return.

Even though I did not know how I was going to stand upright, let alone work after this, I needed to get away from him.

From everything.

Far, far away.

He pulled up behind the nursing home where I worked, and I jumped out without looking back. He squealed off as soon as my door shut. I collapsed in the parking lot by the dumpster and sobbed.

When I finally felt strong enough to stand, I walked over to the door which led to the basement locker room, but instead of opening it I pulled out his flip phone and dialed the number I knew by heart since I was a child.

"Aunt Victoria, I need your help."

Chapter Two

Victoria

"VICTORIA, are you telling me you haven't told your sister you have cancer and your niece just randomly called you and wants to stay with us for the winter of all months? Does she know how cold it gets up north?"

Troy had a point. The whole thing was a little ironic, but I knew my sister Diane could not possibly be behind it. When was the last time Lizzy called me? She had to be close to twenty-four now. Something seemed wrong.

"I have told no one in my family, but Lizzy seemed really upset about something. She didn't say what or why."

"You don't think your sister had anything to do with this? Having her call you?"

I shook my head at the thought. "I don't think so. My mom would have called me, and I don't think Lizzy has contacted her in quite some time."

Lizzy and my sister had not been on the best of terms since Lizzy's father passed away from a sudden heart attack when she was fourteen. My sister hit the bottle hard and moved in with my parents. My poor niece struggled so much, and my sister selfishly only thought about how the accident affected her. She stopped being a mother to Lizzy during the time she needed her mom the most.

"With all our traveling for work, I felt like I abandoned them. I wasn't there as much as I should have been after he died."

"Babe, you were there as much as you could be. You wanted to help your sister, but she needed to help herself. She still does. She has a drinking problem, and your parents were there for her, so it wasn't like she was alone." He squeezed my shoulders. "You're not responsible for this, you hear me? Your sister is ill, and it's not your fault."

No, it was partially my fault. I could have called more, helped with Lizzy more. My sister and my niece had been through so much, and I was busy working and trying to escape it all. I came back when I found out I was sick, but I was too afraid to tell them about my cancer. I wasn't sure my family could handle my diagnosis. They had to deal with enough as it was. And I feared it would push my sister over the edge.

"Maybe it's time you told your family and definitely Lizzy since she will be staying here."

I shrugged my shoulders.

Troy would never understand the dynamics of my relationship with my sister or the effect this would have on my parents. My sister could hardly hold herself up, let alone take on my obstacles. She had not dealt with the grief after Zach died. She would rather numb the pain.

"Trust me on this one, babe. It's for the best," I whispered. "I'll tell her once there is good news."

He let out a long exhale and turned away. "Fine, but it won't be easy to hide the cancer from Lizzy when she's staying here. What will you tell her when we head to Rochester in a week for the tests?"

"That we're going away together on vacation or something?" I flipped my hair behind my shoulder. "I don't know. I'll think of something. We don't need to worry about it today."

He came up behind me and rested his head on my shoulder. I spun around and clasped my hands behind his neck. "Don't you worry about it, okay? Let me handle my family."

He glanced down, his face etched with worry.

I gently lifted his chin, and our eyes locked. His gaze was filled with fear and concern.

"You need to stop worrying so much, okay? Worrying won't help anything," I said. "We need to appreciate every day together and live our life to our fullest. Nothing has really changed, right?"

He forced a smile, and I smiled as joyfully as I could to show him I was okay. "Troy, everything will be okay. The scans will be perfect and the doctor will tell us the cancer is gone, and we can go back to the way things used to be."

My vision of the future was close to impossible, but we could only hope.

The cancer had been spreading, and I knew I needed a miracle for the cancer to be gone, but I'd be satisfied with no change since the last scans. My outlook wasn't good.

He ran his fingers through my thin hair. My stomach was in knots at the thought of him accidentally pulling more of my hair out. Even though I wore the cold cap religiously when I went through chemotherapy, my hair was thin. The cap was uncomfortable and cold when I had to wear it and I had horrible headaches and a chill that was so intense it was painful, but all the challenges were worth it to save my hair.

He pulled me in for a deep, intense kiss. A longing and desire for what we once had left me with goosebumps and a smile when our bodies finally parted. I wanted that back. I wanted to feel again. I grabbed him and kissed him again. Nothing else mattered in this moment but the breath we shared.

I rubbed my nose with his once we pulled away again and closed my eyes, our foreheads now rested together.

"I love you," I whispered, trying to hold back the tears. "It's going to be okay. I'm not going anywhere, okay?"

"Promise me when we get the news you're in remission, you will tell your family."

"Baby, when I get good news we'll throw a big party and I'll invite all my family, okay?"

"Okay," he said, smiling at the thought. "But you aren't cooking."

Before cancer, I was at the gym five days a week. We both had jobs, traveling all over the world and living a carefree life. After the diagnosis, all that changed. We stopped traveling and bought Troy's parents' cabin in Side Lake, right on beautiful West Sturgeon Lake. His brother, Kevin, lived next door with his wife, Lyndsey. We quickly became best friends, and we reunited with old friends and got to know new friends, too.

My long runs became walks, and my walks now only happened on days I had enough strength.

The change from living in the most glamorous and beautiful places in the world to living in a rural lake town in the middle of the woods was quite an adjustment at first, but the quietness of this past year was exactly what I needed to deal with the side effects of chemotherapy.

The weakness and vomiting had me laid up many days. Troy would make up a bed for me on the deck looking over the lake to breathe in the fresh air. I would listen to the sound of cheering as water-skiers and wake-boarders did tricks behind the boats and the happiness of families coming together to spend their weekends at the lake.

The scenery and atmosphere was meditative and relaxing. I loved napping on a towel in the sand, an umbrella shading me from the sun. Even a few minutes in the sun during chemo left me with a terrible sunburn I learned rather quickly. My skin was always dry, itchy, and red. The palms of my hands and the bottoms of my feet were cracked and swollen but they were slowly healing since my last chemo treatment three months ago. Yet, I seemed to get weaker and more exhausted.

September had arrived with a definite chill in the air. I was cold all the time now, and the fall wind made me even colder.

I was excited to see my niece and spend time with her. We lost touch too long ago, and I wanted to get to know the adult Lizzy.

My family moved to St. Paul just after I graduated from high school. I stayed in Side Lake at the Pine Beach campground and would visit them sometimes.

My sister was a few years older than me and by the time I graduated from high school, she was pregnant with Lizzy. Diane and Zach were so in love and had so many plans. Just fourteen years later, he was gone, just like that. He was too young to die.

My sister had not been much of a drinker before that, and we all made excuses for her as she numbed the pain. We thought she just needed some time. She had been through so much.

My parents invited Diane and Lizzy to move in with them so they could save money and it was obvious my teenage niece needed more structure in her life than my sister could give her. Time passed and Diane's drinking got worse and she avoided dealing with her feelings.

She'd been to rehab three times now. Once out, she would go back to drinking. It destroyed her relationship with my niece and hurt our relationship, too. My sister blamed me and said I wasn't there for her when she needed me. Maybe it was true, but I couldn't bear to watch her destroy herself. I hardly even recognized her anymore.

For us, we had a hard time understanding why she would not go to therapy, or why after being sober for a month, she would start drinking again. It felt like she was not trying at all.

Lizzy moved out the day she turned eighteen and hooked up with Dalton. I met Dalton a couple times, but he always answered for Lizzy when I tried to talk with her. He was obviously controlling and abusive, but she would not listen when my parents and I both tried talking with her about him.

She distanced herself from her mother and stopped coming around. I never blamed her, but my heart broke for her. She stopped answering my calls, too. It was devastating, but there was nothing I could do until she was ready to reach out again.

This phone call was out of the blue, but I was glad she finally called. My sister and I were not close anymore, and when I saw her, we would fight about her drinking. Regardless of the time of the day, she was drunk and a mean drunk at that.

Our close knit family broke apart, and my parents gave up trying to help her. They provided a roof over her head, and she did what she wanted. She struggled to hold down a job and never had any money. But my parents knew she would not survive on her own. I never wanted to give up on my sister, but I had enough.

One day I called her and just lost it on her. I was upset Lizzy was not calling me back and worried about what she was going through. I was too far away to do anything, and I refused to involve my parents. They were old, and they were doing enough already.

Diane would not listen to me and refused to admit Dalton was anything but perfect for Lizzy. I told her she was a worthless drunk. She called me a selfish brat and we stopped talking to each other after that.

It hurt. She was supposed to be there to protect her daughter. Instead, she was too wrapped up in her next drink.

I still saw her on holidays and went to visit my parents in the cities when I could, but I would only get angry when I saw a bottle in her hand every time I was there.

My heart broke for Lizzy. She lost her mother and her father.

My heart was heavy, plus this upcoming doctor's appointment had me on edge. I was afraid of what the doctor would tell me.

My friends knew I had cancer. Troy's family knew and were supportive, but I could not get myself to tell my family. It just wasn't the same. My sister struggled with grief and my parents had enough on their plate dealing with Diane's alcoholism and impulsive behavior. The longer I put off telling them about my cancer, the harder it became to tell them. What would I say? I was hiding my cancer for months.

It wasn't just my family I had been lying to. When the doctor was concerned about some of my symptoms after the chemo, and told me he thought it was spreading, I put off going in for more tests. I was worried about what he would find. Instead, I put off the appointment three times and prayed for a miracle. I told Troy the doctor said it was getting better. I just couldn't let him down by telling him the truth.

Chapter Three

Lizzy

"ARE you sure you're okay taking the bus? Do you even have any of your stuff? Let me at least pack you a bag of my clothes," Ava said.

She looked more nervous than I felt about me leaving. I did not want to take Ava's stuff, but she was trying to help me. She needed to help me.

"Fine, you can pack me a small bag, but just a couple shirts and a pair of jeans. I don't mind being in my scrubs," I said.

She wiped her tears and opened her closet door. "What do you want me to tell Dalton if he comes looking for you?"

"That you haven't seen me," I mumbled.

She nodded and put a shirt, a pair of pants, and her hair brush in my bag.

"Ava, you don't need to give me your good hair brush."

She turned around and handed me the bag. "Are you kidding me? It's the least I can do." She grabbed my hands. "I wish I could do more."

I smiled and wiped my eyes with the back of my hand and sniffled.

"I'm proud of you for leaving him. I know it can't be easy. You'll be much happier in the long run, but I'm going to miss you."

I hugged her, squeezing her extra tight. "Thank you so much for being such a good friend. I'll be back to see you when things settle down."

Her eyes lit up with hope. "Promise?"

"I promise."

"You'll call me when you get there?"

I laughed. "You know I don't have a phone, but I'll find a way."

She'd seen me throw my flip phone in the toilet after I called my aunt. I was not giving Dalton a way to find me.

"Just take care of yourself and call me if you need anything. I don't care what it is. Promise?"

"Yes, I promise," I said. "Don't worry so much about me. I'm going to be fine. My aunt is nothing like my mother."

I had two hundred dollars left to my name after the bus ticket and the taxi to my aunt's house in Side Lake. Was Dalton out looking for me? Did he put down his game long enough to notice I never came home?

I was terrified to ever step foot in that house again. Terrified the druggies would be back to kill us. I was even more worried about the money Dalton probably owed someone for the drugs they stole. How did I let myself get involved with him? How did I fall in love with him?

The curtains shifted, and my aunt's head poked out the door. "Lizzy? Lizzy, is that you?"

She walked up to me as soon as I shut the taxi's door and smothered me in a giant hug. Her body was so frail, her face so much thinner than I remembered.

I hugged her back, but it felt a little awkward. I was different since I last saw my aunt. Numb, broken, and scared for tomorrow. Everything about me changed in just a few years.

Our hug seemed so heavy, an exchange of our emotions. I felt her body tremble beneath mine, and she let out a sigh of relief.

My body relaxed in her arms, and my eyes watered until I was full out crying. In an instant, I was shaking and sobbing in her arms like a child. I tried to turn it off, but it was too late.

"I'm here," she whispered in my ear. "Let it out. I'm here." She was crying, too.

Our hug spoke to each other more than our words could. I was struggling to breathe now. My nose was running all over her sweater, and I was apologizing and wiping my eyes, but she did not seem surprised at all. There was this calmness to her.

Crying felt good, and the way it felt to be held by someone who truly made me feel safe and wanted in such a brief embrace. When was the last time someone actually held onto me like this?

I pulled away. "Sorry, I don't know what got into me. It was a long drive and a long bus ride."

She held my shoulders at arm's length and smiled at me. "It's great to see you, Lizzy. I'm so glad you're here. It's been too long. We need to catch up." She looked behind me. "Oh no, did you forget your stuff in the taxi?"

Here we go. "Not exactly. There...ugh...was a fire and my stuff didn't make it, so it's just me."

"What! I did not know. A fire? How scary," she said. "Why didn't you say anything? You poor thing." She threw her hands up in the air and hugged me again.

My aunt was always an over emotional person.

"I'll take you shopping, and we'll buy you some new clothes, okay?"

Was she for real? She was taking me shopping? I had found my very own fairy godmother. I knew she was rich, but I was not expecting her to buy me a bunch of new clothes.

The guilt ached in my chest, but I could not tell her the truth. Not only would it worry her even more, but I did not want her to think less of me.

My grandma told me Aunt Victoria was going through some stuff and she worried it was divorce. Hopefully, the arguing between them would not get too bad while I was living with them. That was not something I needed right now. I'd have to find another place to stay and my options were pretty slim at the moment.

Victoria led me inside. "I made up a bed for you in one of the guest bedrooms. Are you tired? Hungry?"

I shook my head. "I just ate." I lied, but I could not eat right now though I could not remember the last time I ate. I was exhausted and needed the closest place to rest my head.

Troy stood up from his stool at the granite breakfast bar and said hello awkwardly. He was trying so hard to look happy to see me, but he was obviously wary of why I was there and if my intentions were pure. Definitely not a divorce. Not the way the guy looked at my aunt with those lovesick eyes. Maybe it was an infertility issue. Whatever it was, it would come out eventually.

"Hey," I said back, my eyes searching the room behind him. The walls were bare, and the room held minimal furniture, like no one was living there at all. Now I was even more curious.

"Honey, will you show Lizzy to her room?" Victoria said to Troy. "I'm going to check on the apple pie."

A fresh apple pie? I was sure that was a candle I was smelling. She was the real deal. My mother always said Aunt Victoria was high maintenance, so I wondered if she had a maid or someone who made the pie for her and she was just taking it out of the oven. But my mother lied about a lot of things and this was likely one of them. My aunt had flour on her pants and a little in her hair. She had baked the pie herself.

Maybe I was just a little hungry.

I followed Troy into the back bedroom, which was smaller than I expected, but still much bigger than the room we had at our duplex.

The bed was all made up with a silky teal comforter and teal and black curtains to match. A teal lamp sat on top of a big white dresser. The closet doors were the pull open kind. I opened the closet door to find a big walk-in closet that would easily fit everything I ever owned in it and then some.

I peeked in the open door and found a small bathroom with a toilet, ceramic sink, and a small shower in it.

"You have your own private bathroom in here, so you don't have to share. I can get a mirror and some shelving in here for all your stuff. Sorry, we just remodeled and we're not quite finished.

He wrinkled his forehead, deep in thought and glanced at my feet. "Wait a minute. Where is your stuff? The living room?"

"No, I, um, lost everything. There was a fire and—"

His eyes widened, and he let out a gasp of disbelief. "Oh geez. I'm sorry. Victoria never said anything."

I shook my head and looked away to hide the guilt on my face. I hated lying. "I didn't tell her until I got here. I just needed to get away, and it hurts to talk about it."

He waved his hands. "I'm really sorry. Do you know what started it?"

His voice held no judgment. "I'm not sure."

Simple and right to the point. I did not need to explain anything or think on my feet.

He headed for the door. "Please, make yourself comfortable and come out whenever you're ready. I put fresh towels in the basket in your bathroom, so feel free to take a shower." He turned back to me. "Oh, and you'll find shampoo and conditioner in there, too."

"Thank you," I forced a smile. "I think that is exactly what I need right now. I can still smell the smoke in my clothes." Cigarette smoke, that is. I would never admit that to them, though.

Maybe the apple pie would wait until morning. A shower was about all I could handle right now.

Chapter Four

Victoria

"SHE WAS THERE when the fire happened? She didn't tell me that." I bit my lip. "Was anyone hurt? She probably inhaled smoke and could need oxygen or something."

Troy grasped my upper arms. "Honey, don't get ahead of yourself. She seems okay. I haven't heard her cough once."

"True. I guess *This Is Us* was just flashing in my head when the dad died from the smoke and..." I waved. "Never mind. I'll try to relax. Thank you for being so nice to her. She's a good girl, she really is."

He kissed me on the lips. He knew I was worried about Lizzy, and that was partly because my sister had checked out so long ago.

"Okay, babe," he whispered. "Let me know what you need and I'll support you one hundred percent. I'm sorry I second guessed her intentions."

I stood up a little taller and pushed my shoulders back. There was nothing sexier then a man who apologized when he was wrong. "Thank you."

Hopefully, I was right, and her intentions were pure. Why would they not be? What did she have to gain from being here and spending time with us? She'd never asked me for anything before.

"I was thinking about my check-up next week, and I was hoping maybe you could stick around with Lizzy while I go to the appointment."

He deadpanned. "You don't want me to come with you? Babe, you talked me into missing the last one. I don't want to miss another one."

The one I rescheduled and instead hung out at Barnes and Noble in the Cities so I could procrastinate a little longer.

I was a fraud.

"Babe, you're the one who keeps saying it's no big deal and to keep thinking positive. I'll be okay. I want to do this by myself."

He shook his head, his eyes pleading with me. "I don't want you to go alone again."

"I can listen to an audiobook and just relax. You know I love my me time. It's just another checkup. We can celebrate the good news when I get home, okay?"

He looked like he was close to crying. I pulled him toward me and kissed his lips again. "It'll be fine, Troy. Trust me."

He rested his forehead against mine and held my hands in his. "Okay. If that's what you want. But promise me this is the last time you'll ask me not to come. It breaks my heart."

"It is. Now, let's cut into the pie."

His eyes lit up. "I thought you'd never ask. I'm starving."

I opened the sliding door and stepped out on the deck after I spotted her sitting in a chair. "Lizzy, you feel up to going kayaking with me?"

Lizzy had been up early. She had started up the coffeepot and even eaten a piece of pie before I crawled out of bed. I noticed her plate in the sink when I stepped into the kitchen.

Troy was still snoring on his side of the bed, not even a stir as I crawled out of bed and put on my robe.

Lizzy jumped when she heard my voice behind her. "Aunt Victoria, you scared the crap out of me!"

I sat across from her on the deck. "I'm sorry. I thought you heard me open the door."

Why was she so startled at my surprised presence? She'd been through a lot, but I did not want to pressure her for answers. It did not matter, anyway. She was safe now, here with me, and I wanted to spend as much time with her as I could.

"I guess I was deep in thought. It's such a beautiful view of the lake from up here." She sighed and her shoulders slouched. "I'm not sure I'm up for kayaking today."

She forced a smile, but the dark rings under her eyes and her swollen eyelids gave away the stress and sleepless nights.

"I promise you'll have a good time," I said. "It's not too windy today, and the leaves are changing. It'll be fun and relaxing in the water. Plus, it's great for the mind. I'm going to keep bothering you until you say yes. I want some time with my niece."

Her lips pressed together in a tight line and a then a soft sigh escaped. "Okay, fine. Why not?"

She gave in so easily. I thought I would have to work a little harder for her to agree.

The September air gave off a cold, wet chill. The water was warmer than the air. Mornings on the lake lately were foggy and beautiful.

I slid my kayak into the water, and Lizzy did the same with hers.

"How do we get into this thing without tipping over?"

"Here, let me help." I held her kayak steady so she could get in.

The water was shallow enough, so she was able to jump in with a little wobble.

I pushed her off shore and climbed into my kayak. I had been kayaking since I was a kid, so I had the process down without tipping.

West Sturgeon was the perfect lake for kayaking. Not only was it the warmest lake on the chain of five lakes in Side Lake, but most of the time the lake was also low on water traffic. When the water level was too high, some boats struggled to make it under the Greenrock Road bridge, which connected West Sturgeon to Big Sturgeon Lake. When the water levels were low, boats sometimes bottomed out. Some boaters lost their props when they went too fast underneath the bridge. That kept them away.

Most of the traffic stayed on the bigger lakes in the chain, so we did not see nearly as many boats over here. It was like a dead end lake on the chain.

West Sturgeon was also my favorite place to waterski because of the calm, warm water, and the cabins and houses around the shoreline were gorgeous to look at. They blended luxury with the natural beauty of the lake. Some had expansive balconies and terraces, others were smaller and well-kept. Half of them were unoccupied during winter and just a summer home. We all watched out for each other, and the summer people had nothing to worry about because the residents kept an eye on their homes.

Although I grew up in the area, I did not know most of my neighbors yet. My husband's brother and his wife, Kevin and Lyndsey, lived next to us and we had some other friends who lived on Turtle Creek Road, but we'd only been living in Troy's childhood cabin for a year now. But we were lucky. His parents were wealthy doctors, and the cabin was bigger than the houses most normal people lived in. The houses in Side Lake sold almost immediately when they were listed.

With all my cancer stuff going on, and the weakness and exhaustion taking over, I had barely been out on the lake at all. All summer I looked out from the porch a lot, but I was too weak to feel the waves in our boat. I went out once and I spent most of the day with my head in the toilet. It took me two days to recover from the nausea.

"Let's head over to the bridge," I said, pointing. My arms were shaking and felt like rubber, but I needed the exercise and time with my niece.

Lizzy had a great pace going, but she was pushing it. She had gotten so thin since the last time I saw her a few years back, although she may say the same about me. I'd been trying to gain weight, but it was so hard after the chemo. Maybe we could try to gain weight together.

Lizzy pointed to a house with a large wooden staircase leading up to the two-story house surrounded by trees that were just slightly turning red and orange. "Some big wig must own that house, huh?"

"Actually, my good friends Kat and Ethan live there. Ethan's a famous author who writes under the name Elizabeth Conrad."

"No way, *the* Elizabeth Conrad? I love her books. His books," she said, correcting herself.

I smiled. Of course, she was a fan. Everyone was a fan. I was glad I could finally make her excited about something. "He's one of our good friends. You will be meeting him soon enough. We are together all the time."

"That is really cool. I love he writes under a female name, but I always wondered why." She stopped paddling to shield her eyes from the sun and squinted at the house, half hidden behind the trees at the top of the hill.

"It's more marketable if a female writes romance than a male."

"That seems weird."

I started paddling again. "I agree, but that's just the way it is. I actually work for Ethan. I design his webpage and do all the updates and marketing when he comes out with new books. Kat and Ethan were childhood sweethearts who lost touch and ended up back together as adults. It's a beautiful love story. They have an adult daughter, Emma, who helps run their bed-and-breakfast."

Once I found out about my cancer and quit my job as a traveling blogger, I worked on marketing and webpages for Ethan to keep me busy, and it did. I never had much energy left at the end of the day, but it gave me something to look forward to. I loved to work and be creative, and he was so great to work for.

"Hmmm. That's cool. Don't you travel anymore?"

I paddled faster, and she followed, but I struggled to breathe. My heart and lungs could not keep up with this strenuous exercise. Nor were my muscles strong anymore.

"No, not anymore," I said as I turned my head away and tried to slow my breathing.

"Are you and Uncle Troy going to start a family or something? Is that why you stopped?"

I hated to lie to her, but the truth was not an option. "Maybe someday. We wanted to move closer to our friends and family, and we wanted to live a life at the lake."

What I said was true. We loved living at the lake, but we would not have made the move so soon. I loved our previous life.

"Even with the frigid Minnesota winters?" She paused. "My mom always told me you both hated the winters up north and you couldn't wait to get away."

She was not wrong. "Yes, we did, but Side Lake has so much to do in the winter."

She eyed me suspiciously.

"Really."

She raised her eyebrows. "Like what?"

I paddled faster to get in front of her so she could not see my face. "Cross country skiing on the trails around here, snowmobiling, snow-shoeing, ice fishing, ice skating, sledding—"

"You're telling me you go sledding down a hill in Side Lake?"

I nodded my head and turned the kayak to get closer to the side of the bridge. "I sure do. I go sledding with my friend Maddy and her son David. Also, my friend Whitney and her daughter Brittany come, too." When I'm not dizzy and nauseous and in bed by six or seven, but I was not about to tell her that.

In a few months, I might actually have the energy to go out and have some fun and get some exercise now that I was no longer on chemo. I always thought I wanted to be skinny, but boney and weak were not sexy. I missed my curves, my happiness, and just being able to make plans and go out and do something.

"I haven't been sledding in years. Is it as exciting as it was when you were a kid?"

I splashed the water in front of her and drops splashed her face. "Stick around and you may find out."

"Aunt Victoria, you're going down," she said as her paddle hit the water and drenched us both.

Chapter Five

Lizzy

MY AUNT ENDED up being a lot of fun. She made me forget about my crappy, awful life for a little while and enjoy nature and feel the peace at the lake. She was even friends with one of my favorite authors of all time. She was so much different from my mother. If only I'd been around her more.

Now if I could just figure out what I would do with the rest of my life. I could not live with my aunt and uncle forever. But right now, living with them sounded appealing. When was the last time I just relaxed without a worry in the world? And kayaking. Who knew I would love kayaking so much? It was a really great workout, too.

I sat at the end of her dock and stared at the water and the trees and everything in nature held right in front of me. The leaves were changing, and the lake was quiet. Just a few waves rushed to shore. I closed my eyes to feel the cold air on my face. It blew a chill right down the back of my shirt, leaving me with goosebumps and a shiver.

The distant noise of an engine roaring by the bridge caught my attention. From the distance, I was pretty sure it was a jet ski. As it drew closer, I saw a man with brown hair and blond highlights. He looked just like Jason Lewis from *Sex in the City 2*, from this far away, anyway.

Goosebumps reappeared on my arms when he looked my way and waved. I lost my breath but waved back as I stuck my feet in the water at the end of the dock. He pulled up at a dock a few doors down and cut the engine. I looked over my shoulder to peek at him again.

He tied the jet ski to the dock and stood up. He shook his head to brush away the water that was dripping into his eyes and ran his fingers through his hair to slick it back and out of his face.

He unzipped his wet suit and let it hang at his waist. I gulped at his ripped chest. But he slipped on a white t-shirt and spoiled my view. He glanced my way in the process, and I looked away a little too fast.

He was still staring my way when I took a peek, so I got up and walked over to him to stop the awkwardness of it all.

"We seem to be the only two people on the lake, so I figured I'd come introduce myself." I held my hand out. "I'm Lizzy."

He stared at me, his eyes curious, before shaking my hand. "Tim."

I could tell the guy was cocky just by the way he tried too hard to smile, all sexy-like. He must be used to getting a lot of women with that smile.

I stuck my hands in my back pockets, not knowing where else to put them, so I wouldn't fidget. "Nice to meet you."

"You just move here or are you visiting?"

I cleared my throat. "I'm staying with my Aunt Victoria Finney." I pointed at her house.

"I thought you may know her when I saw you on her dock. It's nice to meet you." His blue eyes were so bright and they glowed like they were not real.

"You know my Aunt Victoria?"

He smiled at me again and bit his lip. "I know Maddy and Brad and they've talked a lot about your aunt, but I haven't met her yet. I just moved here a couple of weeks ago."

I wrinkled my brow at him. "Who is Maddy?"

"What?"

"I'm not from around here and I'm not sure who Maddy is."

"I can't believe you don't know Maddy," he said.

"My aunt has talked about her friends, but I haven't met any of them yet. How do you know Maddy?"

A mischievous smirk spread across his face. "I work with them."

He was mysterious, and I was not sure whether I liked or despised him.

"Troy Finney is your uncle, correct? Kevin's brother?"

I nodded. "I believe that's his brother's name. Victoria is my aunt and I'm here visiting for a few weeks. I live in the Cities."

"Oh, okay," he said with a nod. As if it all made sense to him now.

"What was the cocky grin all about, anyway?" Straight to the point. I had to show him he did not intimidate me with that relaxed swagger and magnetic energy. No way. I'd show him.

He crossed his arms and lifted an eyebrow. "What cocky grin?"

I shook my head at him. "Oh, don't give me that. You aren't fooling anyone."

He raised his hands in surrender, which really got under my skin.

"I'm a teacher and I used to work at the elementary school with them when I first started teaching. Now I'm in the high school. You are brutal."

I tapped my foot. "Why do I get a feeling you aren't telling me everything?"

"It's a long story, but let's just say Brad and I started off on the wrong foot, but now we're buddies. They called me about six months ago and told me someone was putting their house on the market on Turtle Creek Road, so I made the couple an offer before they found a real estate agent. Two months later, I moved in. Can't get any better than a lake town in northern Minnesota."

I gave him the stank eye.

"That's it. I promise."

It was hard to tell if he was still pulling my leg or if he always gave off arrogant vibes. For some reason, I believed him. "I wonder if you'll still feel that way when it's winter," I said.

"I've been working in Hibbing for a few years now. I don't mind the cold. Plus, nothing beats a fireplace, and I can't wait to try out mine when it gets cold enough."

I had to remind myself to look away. I kept staring into those beautiful, devilish blue eyes. Were they aqua? Teal? Turquoise? No, more like the color of the sky on a clear day.

The silence had become awkward. I cleared my throat and tried to remember what he just said to me. Keep it together, Lizzy. He would not intimidate me with his unflattering charm.

"Are your aunt and uncle home? I'd like to introduce myself to them," he said.

"Nope," I said. He was not following me into the house. "I was just leaving."

He eyed me curiously. A smirk slowly spread across his face. "I thought I saw their cars up there," he said.

"Nope," I replied with no emotion.

"Okay, then. What is it you do for a living, Lizzy?"

My jaw tightened. "I'm in between jobs."

"Well, I can tell I've said something to upset you. I'll stop asking you questions."

I stepped back.

"I'm sorry if I said something that offended you. It was nice to meet you," he said, all too innocent.

I turned around and glared at him, then walked away.

"Let me make it up to you," he said.

I turned around. "Are you kidding me? Are you for real right now?"

He smiled and leaned back casually, flashing me those perfect white teeth. "You're new to town, right? Let me take you to dinner at Highway Five for their fish fry, and if you still think I'm a jerk by the end of the evening, I'll never trouble you again."

I shook my head. "Not happening, Tim."

"Then I'll come up and meet your aunt and uncle instead. Maybe hang out for the rest of the evening."

Oh no, he wouldn't. I turned again to flash him an intense glare. "You aren't hanging out with us."

He shrugged. "Then let me take you to dinner."

I let out another frustrated groan. "Fine, you win, but if I don't like you by the end of dinner, you won't come over again."

"Deal," he said. "Pick you up at five?"

I threw my hands up in surrender to show him how I really felt about this. Why did I give in?

I'm not sure why I said yes, but I already regretted it. He was a cocky jerk who struggled to take no for an answer. He tricked me. It all happened so fast.

Chapter Six

Victoria

"TIM AND YOUR NIECE, huh? He is a great guy," Maddy said. "Brad and I had just gotten divorced when Tim was subbing for Whitney at the school after she broke her leg."

Maddy smiled as she recalled the memory. "Tim was gorgeous and sweet and so charming. We enjoyed a moment or two of lust and flattery, but in the end, Brad was the only guy for me and Tim and I ended up becoming great friends."

I hadn't known Brad and Maddy divorced, but Troy told me that after their daughter died, they went through a rough patch. They were such a great couple, and their marriage was so uplifting now. I'd never know.

"And how does Brad feel about him now? Does he know you and Tim had a fling?"

Maddy laughed. "It's a long story, but he and Brad actually got into a fight and Tim put Brad out flat on his back in the hallway at the school." She shook her head at the memory. "Brad was jealous, so it wasn't like Tim was aggressive or anything. Brad definitely deserved it. They're good friends now."

"That shows how strong your marriage is," I said. "I was planning on having a fire tonight and inviting everyone so Lizzy could get to know our friends, although it looks like they beat me to the introductions."

Maddy's eyes lit up. "I can't wait to meet your niece. What's she like?"

"Well, to be honest, I haven't seen her in years and we're just getting to know each other again. Her father passed away when she was a teenager and my sister kind of went off the rails with her drinking. Lizzy got lost in the shuffle," I said. Guilt consumed me when I thought about it. "My sister and I don't exactly see eye to eye, so she doesn't talk to me very much."

"That's so sad. How did he die?"

"Heart attack." I paused. "He was too young."

"That's horrible."

"Everything went downhill after that so I was surprised that one day out of the blue Lizzy called and said she had a fire at her house and she wanted to stay with me for the winter."

Her mouth fell open. "A fire? That's terrible. Did she get hurt?"

I shrugged. "I don't really know a lot of details. She doesn't like to talk about it, but it sounds like she was okay. She doesn't know about my cancer though, and I want it to stay that way until I hear more from my doctor on the progression."

Maddy put her hand on mine. "I won't say a word. I have a feeling you'll receive good news though. When will you find out?"

"Next week."

"Oh, wow." Maddy frowned, and worry reflected in her brown eyes. "Are you feeling okay about it?"

"Yeah. I haven't had any problems or concerns other than the normal aches and pains and exhaustion, but it's slowly getting better."

"And it will only continue getting better," she said.

Lizzy walked in and sat down next to me.

"Hi, I'm Lizzy. What will continue to get better?"

"Lizzy, this is Maddy, the friend I was telling you about. Maddy's husband Brad is Lyndsey's brother."

"And Kevin is Uncle Troy's brother, correct?"

She had a great memory. It was so nice having her around. I missed having family close.

"Yes." I turned to Maddy. "Maddy, Lizzy, Lizzy, Maddy."

"Hello, Lizzy. It's so great to finally meet you. I've heard so much about you," Maddy said with a welcoming smile.

Maddy had that way with people. She was always so friendly and kind. The minute I met her, we bonded instantly.

"I've heard about you, too. Not only from my aunt but Tim mentioned he knew you," Lizzy said, looking a little nervous.

"I heard the two of you are going to a fish fry tonight. Tim is a great guy. You'll have a lot of fun."

Lizzy shook her head. "I'm not into him like that. We're just friends."

I cleared my throat. "Maddy is having people over tonight for a bonfire and then we're all going to hot tub at Kevin and Lyndsey's if you feel up for it after your friend date."

"I'd love that," she said with a laugh.

"Bring Tim. I texted him, but maybe you want to remind him."

She avoided my eyes. "Sure."

What was she up to? Did she have feelings for Tim or did she hate him? It was hard to tell.

Lizzy went upstairs to get ready for her *friend* dinner date, and Maddy and I went out to the back deck, wrapped ourselves up in fleece blankets, a glass of wine in our hands.

"It's sure chilly out here. I can't believe Tim was jet skiing earlier. Wetsuit or not, it's too cold for that," I said.

"You don't know Tim. He's a risk-taker, a free spirit. He's athletic and loves to do things to get a reaction. I have a feeling your niece is going to fall fast."

Considering how down Lizzy had been, I was hoping Maddy was

31

right. But I also worried Tim would break her heart and then she would leave.

If he was as good looking as Maddy made him seem and if he had a heart like she described, Lizzy was in trouble. She'd been through more heartache than she should at such a young age. I did not want to see her hurt when she came here to spend time with me. But there was nothing I could do. I would not get in between them and try to stop anything from happening. They were no longer children, and she had to learn somehow. I shook away my thoughts when the doorbell rang.

Maddy jumped up, and I followed her to the door.

"Tim!" she said. "How are you?"

He wrapped Maddy in a tight hug and kissed her cheek. "Well, if it isn't Mrs. Jones. I did not expect you to be on the other side of this door. What a pleasant surprise."

"Yeah, well, Victoria is a good friend of mine and Lizzy is her niece," Maddy said.

He bobbed his head. "That's what Lizzy said."

"I'm sorry," Maddy said. "I should properly introduce you two. Tim, Victoria. Victoria, Tim."

He extended his hand to me. "Nice to finally put a face to the name."

I squeezed his hand back while staring at his unique light blue eyes. He was quite a handsome man. A heartbreaker, for sure.

"Same," I said, raising my wineglass in his direction.

He looked back at Maddy. "Maddy, I got your text. Hot tubbing and a fire, huh? Sounds perfect. Lizzy and I are going to the fish fry and then we'll be there. I'm not sure Lizzy will want to put up with me very long, anyway."

Maddy laughed. "I'm sure she'll manage. The fish fry will win her over."

"That's true. The Highway Five Bar and Grill Friday night fish fry was the real reason I moved out to the lake," he said with a wink.

Oh, he had charm alright.

We all turned when Lizzy walked into the room. She looked gorgeous in my black tank top with a red and black checkered flannel, half buttoned up and a tight pair of jeans. She wore makeup for the first time since her arrival. I told her to pick something out of my closet and use my makeup and curling iron if she wanted, and I was glad she took me up on it. Her hair hung down her shoulders in a beach wave and her eyes sparkled.

Tim whistled. "You look great." I watched as he slowly scanned her body from head to toe, glancing away as soon as her eyes caught his.

He did everything but drool as he took in her appearance. This was no doubt a date, despite what Lizzy said.

Tim took Lizzy's hand and pulled her to him as they made their way out the door.

"I can walk just fine," she said.

Sassy and independant.

I raised an eyebrow and looked at Maddy.

"See you later," he said. "If she doesn't strangle me before we come back."

I laughed at the banter between them. Was this anger real, or was it the way they flirted with each other?

I shook my head at Maddy and laughed. "You aren't kidding. He's a handsome young guy, isn't he?"

Maddy smiled. "I lied earlier. I actually met him before he became a substitute teacher. My friend Whitney and I went rock climbing in Duluth. Tim was the rock-climbing instructor. He had all the women's heads turning, let me tell you."

"I can see that. He's much younger than I thought he'd be."

We sat back on the balcony. I pulled my blanket around me again, my glass of wine tucked just inside the opening.

"Yeah, he's much closer to Lizzy's age than mine. I like to call it my mid-life crisis, triggered by grief."

We both laughed.

I stood up with my empty wine glass in my hand. "More Cabernet?"

"Yes, please. You read my mind."

Chapter Seven

Lizzy

WE SAT DOWN and ordered drinks. An older blonde woman came up to the table and spoke to Tim. "It's Tom, right?" She held onto the back of the chair and seemed to have a hard time keeping her footing steady.

"It's Tim. How are you, Lisa?"

He did not seem thrilled to see her, but l he did his best to stay casual. "I'm doing good. Real good. The last time I saw you, you were chasing a much older woman and now here you are with this high schooler? At least she's a little closer to your age."

"Lisa, this is Lizzy and she's been out of high school at least a couple of years now," he said.

The waitress set our drinks in front of us.

Lisa waved at the waitress. "Oh, miss, did you card this child?"

The poor waitress wrinkled her forehead. "Excuse me?" She looked around, as if trying to figure out where the child was.

Lisa stepped in and loudly whispered for all the surrounding tables to hear and pointed t me. "I don't think this girl could be a day older than nineteen. I just want to make sure you don't get in trouble." She turned and looked back and forth between Tim and me. "You aren't a cop, are you?" she said in an attempt to be bratty.

Before Tim could jump to my defense, the waitress said, "Yes, she's been carded. Maybe you should return to your table and leave them be."

The waitress was not a fan, either. Who was this, Lisa? I was dying to hear. Small city politics could be entertaining. Tim had only lived at Side Lake like a month. How did he already have enemies? Did he struggle to get along with people?

The waitress left, and Lisa stuck her hand out in front of me. I took the bait and shook it.

"Lizzy," I said. "And you must be Lisa."

"Sure am. You've heard of me, huh? The entire school has probably been buzzing about me. I imagine the school probably fell apart after I left. I did everything there. I can't imagine what it's like now. Although, you're just a sub, aren't you, Tim? You probably don't even know."

He stood up. "Actually, I'm a stripper now. I can't believe you didn't know."

She gasped, and her eyes widened. "A what?"

I had to bite my lip to keep from laughing.

"A stripper, well, when I'm not an escort, that is. Is that why you came over to say hello? I know you've struggled with male attention." He paused. "Married men, correct? Is that going any better for you? I heard you're looking for a job. Give me a call and I'll see if there are any openings. Then again, you'd probably have to remove the stick from your butt first."

He said that all with an amiable smile, and I had to turn away and cover my mouth to hide my amusement.

Her eyes blazed. "How dare you! You're a disgrace." Lisa sniffed and turned her nose away. "How dare you insinuate that I—"

"Maybe you should listen to the waitress and have a seat. Looks like someone just came in to join you," I said, trying to get her to walk away. We were already attracting too much attention.

She glanced at her table. "Tracey," she said and waved. She turned back to Tim and waved a finger in his face. "And you're a sad excuse for a man. I hope you get your karma someday. Now if you'll excuse me."

"It was great seeing you, Lisa. Enjoy your dinner."

She stomped away, grabbed her purse and Tracey's arm, and stomped her way right out the door.

"I hope she didn't leave without paying her tab," I said.

"Maybe she'll get arrested. That would be so fun to watch."

I shook my head and laughed. "Have you been here long enough for people to hate you that much?"

"She was a teacher at Dylan Elementary in Hibbing when I was a sub. She tried to break up Maddy and Brad but was surprisingly unsuccessful. It's a long story, but let's just say she quit teaching on the last day of school. Then Brad fired her when she tried to come back. Although it may not need to be said, she's an awful woman."

"I could see that. You seemed to have no problem pushing her over the edge." She was rude, and she came at him first, but he continued to egg her on and make a scene which made me wonder if he was a cocky jerk.

"Does she live in Side Lake?" Hopefully she lived nowhere near us. I would not want to run into her again.

He shrugged. "I sure hope not. But enough about her." His expression changed. "Tell me more about you. Your mom and Victoria are sisters, correct? Are they close?"

"That was a quick change of subject." I cleared my throat. "They used to be, but my mom is an alcoholic and struggles with a lot of mental health issues. I don't think anyone is very close to her right now."

"I'm sorry to hear that. At least you have a nice aunt. Victoria seems cool."

"She is. We kind of lost touch after...well, after I moved away from my mom I lost touch with all my family." Why was I telling him all this? The words popped out of my mouth before I could stop them. I had no filter tonight.

"So, you and your mom got into a big fight, and you moved out," he said, summarizing my words. "Now you've moved here to make things right with your aunt? Is that what you're saying?"

"Yeah, I guess I am, but I came here to escape my life in the Cities, and my aunt was the first person I thought to call." I paused. "I guess a part of me wanted to reunite with her and I had a reason to call." I shook my head. "You probably think I'm crazy." I bit my nail and locked eyes with him. "But I don't care. You can think however you want."

"I don't think that at all, but I want to know more about you." His knee brushed against mine under the table, and my heart skipped a beat. Was it an accident or did he do it on purpose? I was rude. Why was he flirting with me?

The waitress took our orders for the fish fry.

"Hey, look, I'm sorry for the way Lisa acted," Tim said. "I hope I didn't embarrass you, bringing all that attention to us. She's just a really terrible person."

"No problem. I thought you were funny. It made me a little nervous, but she brought it on herself." I leaned in closer to him. "Do you think she paid before she left?"

"Yes, the waitress didn't seem too worried about it."

"Well, that's good."

"Otherwise, I would have paid. It wouldn't be right for the waitress to be stiffed."

Lisa's inappropriate behavior was not his fault. But The fact that he felt responsible and would pay her bill said a lot about him. The jury was still out, but I was starting to believe he may be a better person than I first thought.

He flashed me that arrogant lopsided smile.

Nah, he was still a jerk.

But the stripper story was the highlight of the evening. He could make me laugh, I'd give him that much.

I laughed out loud at the thought, and he looked at me sideways, confused but intrigued.

"Sorry, the stripper story gets me."

Tim was appearing kind and refreshing, and I slowly let my guard down. I was not sure whether it was an act, but I would give him a chance. He was a distraction but not really someone I would ever want to date. He was entertaining, and I had nothing to lose by going out to dinner with him this once.

With Dalton, I struggled to get his attention. He treated me like I belonged to him. I never realized how much I hated feeling trapped. I was truly miserable, but I never thought to leave him. The truth was, I was scared. Scared of him, and what he would do. Luckily, Dalton lived far away from Side Lake and he would never think to come looking for me here. He had probably forgotten about me and found a new girl to push around.

Why did the thought hurt?

Tim straightened his chair and reached for his beer. "I find myself curious about you. What were you escaping from exactly?"

He rubbed his scruffy whiskers, and I squirmed in my seat and cleared my throat. "Well, let's just say I was in an unhappy relationship for a very long time and coming here has been a real eye-opening experience."

"I'm sorry to hear that. I've been in a few of them myself." He smiled. "Is that why you came here? To get away from him?"

This was a little too deep for our first date. I hardly knew him, and I'd told him more than I told my aunt.

"Kind of. I'd rather not talk about it. Let's talk about something else."

He nodded and took a drink of his beer. "I want to hear more about you. Tell me something else I don't know."

How to answer such a broad question. "Well, I was a CNA in the Cities. I worked at a nursing home. I thought I hated it until I got here and realized I hated my life there, not being a nurse. My choices." I paused, my heart racing at the thought. "Now I know I want to work with children in the pediatric unit. I want to make a difference."

He stood up straighter. "I have nothing but respect for anyone in the medical field, especially since COVID. We live in a whole new world now. I see the passion you have. It's refreshing."

He did not know I was pretty much a drug dealer a few days ago. What would he say if I mentioned I was held at gunpoint? He'd run. He'd definitely run. The thought of that night sickened me. What the hell was I doing in that life with Dalton? I was working as a nursing assistant, but I was not in control of my life or my life decisions. I never saw it before. Funny how a little distance made me see so clearly.

I looked at him with a nervous smile. "I'm really not so sure about you, Tim. I wanted to hate you and then you started acting all nice and caring. You ruined the whole cocky player vibe you had going on."

He leaned forward, so close to my face. "So, you're saying you think I'm a good person then? I'm kind of growing on you?"

He was challenging me in a flirty voice, and I was kind of into it. "I don't know if I'd say good person, but enough to maybe see you again."

The cocky look was back. He leaned forward, and I almost felt him reeling me in like a fish. Ironic.

I shook my finger at him. "Don't get any ideas. I'm not into you. I'm just saying I agree to hang around you sometimes, and I don't mind going out to dinner with you, if you pay that is."

"Sounds to me like you are having a good time."

I was on fire. Being confident and blunt felt good. Not me, the old me, anyway, but I felt light around him. "You still seem egotistical. How is it you became a teacher?"

He pretended to take offense, but he was joking right back with me. He had a good sense of humor. Oh crap, there were too many good things about the guy. That alone had to be a red flag.

"The truth is," he said, leaning in and whispering. "This is all an act. I'm really just a big teddy bear and high schoolers are a challenge because they scare the crap out of me."

A part of me believed he spoke the truth. "They scare the crap out of you. How?"

"If you show any fear, they will eat you alive. Like vultures," he said with a poker face.

I laughed so hard my stomach hurt. I was drawing attention to myself in the small-town restaurant, but for the first time in my life, I did not care. I no longer wanted the night to end.

The server interrupted my thoughts when she brought our food to the table.

The fish looked and smelled delicious. We both ate in silence for the next few minutes. Our tastebuds wanted all our attention as we focused on the taste of each bite. My boneless fish was crispy yet tender and melted in my mouth. Definitely the best walleye I'd ever eaten.

Tim finally looked up at me. "So what do you think? Did I pick a good place?"

"Yes, you did. I'm in awe right now. You northerners are very serious about good food. I've learned to go to Bimbo's for the pizza and wings,

Riverside for their Colorado bulldogs, The Viking for their burgers, Valentini's and Sammy's for pasta, and The Highway 5 Bar and Grill for the fish fry. Am I missing anything?"

"You still have a lot to learn, my young Padawan."

"A *Star Wars* fan. I can respect that." I looked around at the packed restaurant. For being in the middle of the woods, many people had shown up. "Is that why this place is so packed? Everyone is here for the fish fry?"

He smiled. "Yep, you have to get here early to get a table. I told you it's the best fish fry around."

"I want to try all these places. What about bakeries?"

"Well, I think I'll save that for one of our future dates."

I took another bite and smiled at him. Was he asking me out again?

Chapter Eight

Victoria

MADDY HANDED ALL the girls strawberry margaritas in the hot tub while the guys built a roaring fire. I kept looking at my watch to see what time it was. I was hoping Lizzy would get back soon to meet my girlfriends before we got out of the water.

Headlights blinded me for a moment when Tim's car pulled up around seven.

"Lizzy, up here," I said.

Two sets of footsteps tromped up the stairs.

"How was dinner?" Maddy said before I had the chance.

"That fish fry was so good. I was impressed," Lizzy said, looking at Tim.

"You went to the fish fry at Highway Five? They have the best walleye around," Whitney said.

I sat up a little taller in the hot tub. "I guess I should introduce everyone to my niece, Lizzy. I think you all know Tim, right?" I had to raise my voice to be heard over the jets.

"I don't know Tim," Kat said, reaching over the hot tub to shake his hand. "I'm Kat."

"Everyone, this is my niece, Lizzy. Lizzy, this is Kat, Whitney, Lyndsey, and you've met Maddy."

Lizzy waved at everyone. "So nice to meet you all."

"Nice to meet you," they all said back.

"Now, get your swimsuit on," I said. "Tim, the guys are down starting the fire next door. We'll be over in just a bit. We need some girl talk first."

He waved goodbye and left.

Lizzy took off her flannel and tank top. She already had a black bikini on under her clothes instead of underwear.

"Look at you all prepared," Whitney said. "I like her already."

"I didn't want to waste time," she said with a bounce in her step.

I grabbed the strawberry margarita I had waiting for her and handed it to her as she climbed into the tub.

She sat down in between Whitney and me.

"I've heard so much about you, Lizzy," Whitney said. "It's so great to finally meet you. How long are you planning on staying?"

Kat yelled over the bubbles. "Victoria, when are you heading to Rochester?"

I put my finger in front of my mouth to hush her, but Kat did not notice because she followed with, "I just know they are going to say the cancer is gone. And all the hell you were put through with the chemo was worth it after all."

"Cancer?" Lizzy said. She looked my way, her brow furrowed. "Wait, you have cancer?"

"Oops," Kat said, and she turned her head and hid behind her margarita.

I shook my head. "I was waiting to tell you until after I knew I was in remission." I sighed. "But I have breast cancer. I'm okay now, really. I've been done with chemo for a while now."

She gasped. "You had breast cancer, and you didn't tell me? Does my mom know? Grandma and grandpa?"

"No." What else could I say? I made a choice to keep the cancer a secret, but I knew it would eventually bite me in the butt. Everything I did was for someone else, but this time I had thought about what I wanted. I did not regret my choices, but I did feel bad.

"I'm sorry I didn't tell you."

She nodded, obviously hurt. "Are you going to be okay?"

"I'm going to Rochester to find out for sure next week. They'll do some scans to see for sure."

She nodded again, not looking me in the eye.

She was angry, that was easy to see. I hoped she would understand it was what was best for me. None of my friends knew the doctors thought the cancer was growing. Few people knew I even had cancer. My health was my business, and I was not ready to stop believing in miracles.

Lizzy took a sip of her margarita. "Is that why you're so thin?"

I had a lump in the back of my throat as I answered. "Yeah, the chemo took a lot out of me. I still struggle to eat, but it' I'm doing better."

More lies.

"Except that day we brought you burgers from the Viking and you scarfed that sucker down so fast I thought you were going to vomit," Lyndsey said, trying to lighten the mood.

I remembered that day and how sick I was later that night but the burger was so worth it.

Maddy stood up in the hot tub. "Should we leave you guys alone to talk?"

I looked to Lizzy, and she shook her head. "No, I'm still trying to process it. Did you all know?"

They nodded.

"If I could have gotten away without telling anyone, I probably would have. I moved back to Side Lake after I found out because the doctor told me support would be good for me." I looked around at my friends and smiled. "And he was right."

Lizzy had tears in her eyes. I held her hand above the water. "And I'm so glad you came into my life at just the right time so we can celebrate the news of me being cancer free together."

She blinked fast and wiped at the tear that escaped down her cheek. "But what if you aren't cancer free?"

I forced a smile. "I am. I just know it." I really wanted to believe it. That was not a lie.

Lyndsey stood up. "Okay, ladies, who's ready to get dressed and have some s'mores by the fire?"

Everyone stood up with her. The uncomfortable atmosphere made everyone want to flee as soon as they had a good excuse. I did not blame them.

The guys were laughing as I walked up and sat next to Troy. He grabbed my hand and kissed it even though he was still in deep conversation with Ethan.

"Kat was so upset she had to pry the girl's fingers off me," Ethan said, and they both laughed.

Kat appeared with a box of peach alcoholic seltzers in her hand. "What are you guys talking about?"

"Ethan's Midwest book signing in Blaine, remember?"

She rolled her eyes. "I can't believe I had to be the one to stop that girl from wrapping her legs around Ethan and pretty much dry humping him in front of everyone."

I laughed. "Wait. What?"

"Yeah, the book signing was over and this girl jumped on him as he stood. He looked petrified, and he froze. I had to use my loud social worker voice and pretty much rip her off him with my hands. For a little girl, she was scrappy and obsessed."

Ethan shook his head at the memory. "I'm not afraid to admit ,that girl scared the crap out of me. My respect for my wife increased that much more. She had this girl pinned by the arms until the police got there. It was quite the scene."

"I think I'm in the wrong field," Brad said, clearly trying to get a reaction from Maddy.

She glared. "Yeah, if that's happening when you're an elementary school principal that would be a problem."

"A big problem," Kevin said.

Tim walked up with a guitar in one hand and a fold-up camping chair in the other.

"Man, you sing, too? We're all in trouble," Brad said, slapping him on the back.

Tim sat down next to him in the chair. He looked at Lizzy, who sat across the fire from him, and smiled and winked at her. Their dinner must have kicked off something between them. She looked so annoyed when she left for dinner with him but when she came back, I felt the chemistry in the air.

Tim strung his guitar until the single chords became a familiar tune so beautiful it left me with goosebumps. Once he began singing, I teared up. His voice was meant for *The House of The Rising Sun* by the Animals, one of my favorite songs of all time. Even the guys cheered and lifted their beer cans. Us girls smiled and enjoyed every note. The tone of his voice was clear and crisp, powerful yet controlled. Every note hit its mark without a bit of strain, coming out powerful and precise.

As he strummed the last chord and stopped, I let out the breath I was holding in. We all clapped and hooted and hollered. Josh even whistled with his fingers between his lips.

Ethan shook his head. "Man, how did you learn to play like that?"

"And sing like that," Whitney said, her hand over her heart. "Your voice is so raw and heartfelt. I feel so emotional right now."

"You best not be pregnant again," Josh teased.

She flashed him the look of death. He was sleeping alone tonight.

Tim looked so confident and flattered at our words. "My father was in a band growing up. He taught me a thing or two."

Confident but humble. I did not know he had it in him.

"That is a beautiful song," Lizzy said softly. "You sounded so effortless. It's obvious you've been singing for a long time."

"Okay, time for hot rock," Brad said, snapping us all out of our swoon over Tim's singing.

Jealous much?

He grabbed a rock next to the fire and threw it to Kevin.

"Ouch," Kevin said, tossing it to Tim.

"What the hell?" Tim said, throwing it to Ethan.

Ethan dropped it and shook his hands.

"What kind of game is this, anyway?"

"Oh, come on. It wasn't that hot," Brad said. "I'm not that much of an idiot."

"I beg to differ," Maddy said, a grin on her face.

"If it wasn't very hot then why didn't you toss it to your wife?" I asked.

Brad threw his hands in the air with defeat. "You got me.".

Maddy patted him on the back. "I'd kill you. Plus, he knows I have absolutely no hand-eye coordination."

I grabbed a marshmallow and put it on the end of the stick and held it above the fire until it started burning. Just the way I liked to cook my marshmallows. To be honest, I hated to put in the work of making it perfectly brown all the way around.

"How are you doing, babe?" Troy said. No one was paying attention to us. They all had their side conversations going on.

"I'm okay." I was hitting my wall, and he could always tell. "Eat this," I said after taking one small bite and handing him the rest of the sticky, sugary goo.

"You know I hate burnt marshmallows, but I'll eat it for you," he said and leaned in to kiss me.

"Thanks, babe. Too much sugar goes right to my brain and makes me anxious."

He licked his fingers after putting the marshmallow in his mouth. "If you want to sneak away and go to bed, go for it. Your eyes don't look good."

I smiled. He knew me so well. He also knew I found it difficult to disappear when we were with our friends. One thing I learned from being diagnosed with cancer was not to take a minute for granted. Troy and I loved traveling the world and meeting new people, exploring new cultures, but there was nothing like having our own home with good friends surrounding us. My home was here, and this was my family. I never wanted to leave when the fun was just beginning.

"I'll stay out just a little longer. It's so great having Lizzy here." I hesitated. "She knows about, you know."

He leaned closer to me. "What? Knows about..." He cupped his pecks, and I shook my head and laughed at his charades.

"Yes, that," I said, putting his hands down. "Kat mentioned the appointment next week, and that she was sure the cancer was gone. It's my own fault, really. No one except Lyndsey knew I hadn't told my family."

"That must have been a shock."

"It's fine. She took it okay."

I think.

He squeezed my forearm. "Are you okay?"

"Yeah. It'll all be better after I get the good news next week."

Lines of worry appeared on his forehead.

"I know you're worried they'll say the cancer is spreading but I know my body, Troy. It's gone. It has to be."

"Hey, I know it's going to be okay, but I'll still worry until we know for sure. I just think you also need to know there's a slight chance we'll have to fight again."

I wasn't sure I could take another round of chemo.

Chapter Nine

Lizzy

I KNEW something was wrong with Aunt Victoria but I never guessed it was cancer. Although things were not great between my mother and me, I hated she did not know what her own sister was going through. What if she died before my mother had a chance to see her? My mother had not gotten over my father's death so would something like this make her worse? Could she get worse? Was that why Victoria avoided telling her or any of us? I needed to try again to connect with my mother, for me, for us. That I knew.

Finding out Aunt Victoria had cancer was shocking, and it made me angry with her at first, but then after walking to the bonfire, I thought about how hard it must be for her if it hurt me this much. What would happen if I found out I had cancer?

Everyone had high hopes for her to beat the cancer. She could afford whatever treatment available if she still had it. Plus, next week she would know her prognosis, and she was going to tell our family. Everything would be okay. I just had to wait a few more days.

"I haven't laughed that hard in a long time," Tim said, walking me to my aunt's house. "What a great night."

"Yeah, they are fun, aren't they?"

He stopped walking and put his light jacket over my shoulders. His touch made my heart ache for more.

"I thought you might need this. It's chilly tonight. Would you like to take a walk down to the dock with me? Pretty soon the docks will be taken out of the water for the winter. Most are gone Labor Day weekend."

"I'd like that," I said, not ready to say goodnight to him yet.

He led the way to his dock and pulled a blanket out of his boat.

I skidded to a stop. "Was this a setup? You had a blanket ready? Should I be concerned?"

He grinned. "That would have been a better plan. I took the boat out on the lake earlier because tomorrow I'm cleaning it and putting it in storage, but I wanted to go on one last ride. But it was so damn cold I had to put a blanket on my lap."

"How did you not freeze?"

He nodded. "I definitely froze. That wind was brutal. I'm not going to lie."

"I love summer. I wish I got here at the beginning of summer instead of the end. Who comes to live at the lake in September?"

He laughed. "Well, I guess you'll have to stay until the end of next summer so you can experience a Side Lake summer."

I smiled.

We stared into the darkness and looked up at the stars.

"It sure is a clear night," he said, breaking the silence.

"I love hearing the waves and looking across the lake at bonfires." I turned to face him. "So tell me why you left Duluth."

"Because I got a student teaching job in Hibbing."

I raised my eyebrow and looked back into the darkness. "And what's the real reason? I know there are schools in Duluth."

"You really know how to read me, you know that? Okay, I wanted to get away from my old life. Start over."

He intrigued me. I wanted to know everything about him. He was not the person I thought he was when we first met. "Why? Did you have a tough upbringing?"

"No, actually the exact opposite. I have a great, supportive family. I just wanted to be somewhere more rural. Duluth is a great city, but I wanted something quieter, more peaceful so I moved to Hibbing. I loved living in Hibbing, but I always wanted a place on the lake." He bounced on his toes as he stood up. "I just never thought it would happen. I feel grateful every day."

I stayed sitting, still not ready to leave the quiet of the night.

"It's very beautiful here. I'm from the Cities so to me Duluth is small. I know what you mean, though. It's peaceful out here."

"Well, it's getting a bit chilly. Should we head back to your aunt's house?"

He held out his hand and pulled me to my feet. I jumped up and found myself inches from his face. We stared at each other for a long moment, I hated this moment was going to come to end.

He cleared this throat and stepped back. We both turned, but Tim misjudged his footing and fell off the dock. It happened in slow motion, but I had no chance to catch him or I would have fallen in with him.

I covered my mouth. "Oh, no! Are you okay?"

He coughed and let out a loud, "Burr." He pulled himself up on the dock.

I held my breath until I knew he was alright then I laughed. I tried so hard to stop but it was out of my control. The harder I tried to stop the more I laughed. He stared at me without a change in his expression as he grabbed both sides of his shirt and pulled it over his head. "You think that's funny, huh?" he said, a challenge in his voice.

Wow. That was what was hidden beneath his shirt? A trail of brown hair lightly sprinkled across the prominent muscles on his pecks. The trail led down and down and down. My eyes followed it until they stopped because his pants were intercepting my view like a brick wall.

His abs glistened in the moonlight. He had a six-pack, no...counting was not my strong suit at the moment. He had an eight pack of abs, but they were not chiseled like he lived at the gym. Rather, they had a slight layer of flesh over them to show he ate well and worked and played hard.

I could only image the look on my face when he watched me watch him as he unbuttoned his pants. This was going too far, and I needed to stop it for my own sanity. I put my hand out to block my vision more than anything.

"What are you doing?" I said.

He stopped and smirked at me with those straight white teeth and one perfectly imperfect front tooth. And sexy. Was he pretending to be this innocent, or did he really not know how dreamy he was?

"I don't know what you're talking about. I'm cold and wet and I was hoping you would offer to give me my jacket back so I could warm up a little."

His wide, muscular shoulders, his back so broad and defined, had me biting my lip to hold back.

I pulled his jacket from my shoulders and held it out to him, but he made no move to take it from me. Instead, he pulled off his pants, almost falling over as he slipped his leg out.

Whoever invented boxer briefs had to be the smartest human being alive. Not too baggy, not too whitey tightly. I should feel relieved they weren't see-through but a part of me was a little disappointed.

He cleared his throat. "You like what you see?"

A hot flush rose up my neck despite the chilly wind. How embarrassing.

I blinked a few times then covered my eyes with my other hand. I wanted to shade the view. I really did. Instead, I separated my fingers and gave him one more glance.

"I'm sorry, I was just...shocked." I laughed at my reaction. Nothing could pry my eyes away from him. I had to hold on to my arms to stop from reaching out and touching him. Was he real? Why was his body so intriguing to me?

"That was obvious," he said with a mischievous smile. "I should have pulled you into the lake with me."

I looked at him and for the first time realized he was shivering, and his body was covered in goosebumps.

"I think the plans have changed and I'm walking you home," I said.

He did not argue with me, but I was pretty sure he couldn't if he tried. He was so cold his lips were turning blue, but it was hard to tell for sure in the dark.

I put my arm around him and silently scolded myself for the thoughts of slipping my hand beneath his jacket to use my body heat to warm him. We walked the rest of the way in silence. The only sound to be heard was his teeth chattering. I had to bite my lip to keep from saying anything inappropriate or sarcastic. He was just so easy to joke around with.

"Well, this is me," he said, nodding at his front door.

I felt like such a jerk. I hated when men stared at my chest when I talked, and I did the same to him with his half naked body.

He opened the door. "Thanks for walking me home, Lizzy. Have a great night."

He moved to shut his door, but I put my foot in the way to stop the door from closing. His eyes widened, and he stared at my foot as if trying to figure out what just happened.

What was I doing? Shut the damn door. Tell him it was an accident. Don't be needy or vulnerable. Don't give in.

Then I surprised myself by saying, "Can I make you some tea while you shower? It's the least I can do for laughing at you."

His lips turned blue, and they had a dark shade of purple moving in.

He moved aside to let me pass. "Tea is in the kitchen, second cabinet. The kettle is on the stove."

I nodded and kept walking until I reached his kitchen.

He turned around and yelled out to me. "And Lizzy."

I turned back to meet his gaze. "Yeah?"

"Make sure it's caffeine free. I don't think I can take any more excitement tonight."

That was too bad, because excitement was all I could think about.

Chapter Ten

Victoria

I PEEKED at my phone again, eleven thirty at night and she still was not home. I should not be this worried. She had a life before she came to stay with me, but I felt responsible, and I worried about her. Was this what parenthood was like? Is this what mothers had to constantly deal with? Lizzy was in her early twenties, but it seemed like she was still a teenager. Where had time gone?

My sister needed to put the alcohol down and be a mother. Nothing was going to bring Zach back. She needed to deal with the grief and move forward. Be here for the people who were still around and loved her. Be here for Lizzy. She needed her mother.

Who was I to talk, really? I could have reached out to Diane a long time ago and made amends but I didn't. She struggled to admit she had a problem with drinking and therefore refused to get help. A part of me wanted to call her and tell her Lizzy was here and she was safe. But then I'd have to tell her about the cancer and I was not ready to do that. Not until this nightmare was over and I no longer had to see the looks of pity from my friends when I had dark circles under my eyes, or I was exhausted or too weak to get out of bed some days.

No matter how much makeup I put under my eyes, the black bags broke through, tinting my concealer. Not sleeping much was not helping either.

I was too young to have death staring me in the face, and no matter how positive I was or how much I acted happy on the outside, on the inside I was terrified.

I was scared to death the doctor would tell me the cancer continued to spread. Having to process that news was bad enough, but comforting Troy was what scared me the most. Leaving him all alone to go on without me was horrible to imagine.

I downplayed a lot with him. I knew there was a very slim chance I'd be in remission. I made a lot of what the doctor told me sound less serious because Troy was always so worried.

When my feet or hands were cracked, he'd put Vaseline on me and give me a massage. When my skin was dry he'd lather me with lotion, and at night he'd brush my hair after my showers. I was scared to look at all the hair I was losing so I would not look at the brush. He'd clean out the brush before I even turned around so I would not see the damage. He got it, and he was always a step in front of me to solve the smallest of problems that would have me in a panic otherwise.

Troy was my other half, the love of my life. He helped me stay positive but he understood the reality at the same time. If the cancer was gone, I'd love to blare my music all the way home and celebrate with him for the six-hour drive. I would probably scream and cry and be so damn grateful, and he would get it. Except, I knew my dream was nearly impossible, and I didn't want him to be there when I heard the news.

Lizzy finally came home at midnight. She tried to be quiet, but the door squeaked just enough for me to hear her.

I wanted to greet her but that would be too weird. What would I say? I didn't want her to think I waited up for her as if she was a child. I listened as the bathroom door shut and the water turned on and off. The sound of her door shutting relaxed me enough, and I finally fell asleep.

. . .

I was putting on a pot of coffee when I heard her footsteps coming into the kitchen. "Good morning, Aunt Victoria. I hope I didn't wake you last night when I came in. Tim and I sat down by the beach talking, and before I knew it, it was midnight.

I'm sure that was not all they were doing, but their love life was not any of my business. "No, not at all. I'm glad you guys had a good night. You seem really light today, happy. I'm glad to see it."

She looked at me sideways.

"You looked so sad when you got here. I'm not sure what you've been through but it's great to see you smiling again."

Her shoulders slumped. "Oh. Well, I'm fine."

I put a fresh cup of coffee in front of her and surprisingly she drank it black.

"We haven't had a chance to talk since you got here. It's been forever. How are things between you and your mom?"

The sparkle disappeared from her eyes. She looked down at her coffee and blew on it. Clearly avoiding my question.

"Not good. It hasn't changed much. She still refuses to get help, but I haven't talked to her in a very long time. Have you spoken to her lately?"

I shook my head. "No, not really. We got into a big fight a few years ago over her drinking, and she's still pretty upset with me." I put my hands around my cup and took a sip. "I've been thinking a lot about what you said. I'll tell her about the cancer sometime around the holidays. That way, I'll have seen my doctor and I might have some better news for her."

"I don't understand why you want to wait. What if the answer isn't what you expect it to be?" She paused and her eyes widened as if she wanted to take her words back. "I don't mean it that way at all, I just mean—"

"It's okay. I know you didn't mean to come off like that. You're just trying to be realistic, right?"

She smiled, and a look of relief crossed her face. "Yes, it's always good to prepare, in case it doesn't go your way."

I shook my head and laughed. "It's crazy hearing you talk so adult-like. I know you're an adult, but the last time I saw you, you were a child."

"Yeah, well, I had to grow up fast when my dad died, and my mom hit the bottle. I'm just lucky I had grandma and grandpa."

"I'm sorry you went through such a horrible time. I can't make excuses for your mom, but one thing I know is she really loves you. But she's struggling. You know that. She can't get past the grief and her mental health. She's numbing all the pain."

Lizzy crossed her arms. "That doesn't make it okay. I'm her daughter. She needed to step up and take care of me, and she didn't. He was my father. She didn't think I would be hurting too?"

Naturally, I wanted to defend my sister, but Lizzy was right. What could I say? She failed her.

Lizzy shrugged off the conversation. "Anyway, Tim is coming to pick me up around noon. He has a place he wants me to see. Can I borrow some of your workout clothes."

"Of course."

They were moving way too fast, but Lizzy was old enough to make her own decisions. I bit my tongue.

"The whole gang is planning on going to Valentini's in Chisholm if the two of you want to join us. They have the best Italian food around."

She stared off and smiled, looking deep in a daydream. "So I've heard."

Her happiness filled me with joy.

"When did you say you have to go to Rochester?"

"Next week," I said.

She nodded. "Am I coming with you?"

"I think Troy was planning on taking out the dock, and he was hoping you would help him. There's money involved."

Troy would be so angry with me. That was not his plan, but it was now. I needed to do this on my own, and I wanted to avoid hurting her feelings.

Her shoulders slumped, and she looked down. "Oh, okay."

She looked defeated. She was hurt by my words. I felt bad, but this was something I needed to do on my own, but I did not have the strength to explain that to her.

No one understood until they were in my shoes. I needed this.

Chapter Eleven

Lizzy

I KNEW a brush off when it happened. Aunt Victoria was caught off-guard when I suggested coming with her to the doctor. We had no communication for years. Why would I think she wanted me there?

I was trying so hard to connect with her, but too much time had passed. Our relationship was like my relationship with my mother. It would never be the same. But I was not ready to leave. Nope. I had to get to know Tim better and I needed some time to figure out my future.

Something about Tim made me want to run because whatever we had was doomed to fail, but the way he treated me with nothing but kindness and respect had me weak in the knees.

I had not expected to feel this way, but he surprised me. Maybe I'd stay for the holidays, have some fun, and leave before he could hurt me.

Tim said to dress for hiking. I put on a sweatshirt and Victoria's athletic pants and stuffed mittens and a hat into my backpack.

He picked me up at noon and opened the car door for me. He was the first guy to ever shut the car door for me, and I kind of liked it. The gesture was sweet.

Once he got into the driver's seat, he looked over at me, smiled all sexy and said, "Buckle up."

I gave him a questioning look as he pulled into the parking lot across the highway from the Iron Man.

"Ironworld, right?"

"It's actually the Minnesota Discovery Center now. Have you been here before?"

"Nope, but I saw it on my way into Side Lake from the highway, and Troy has talked about it. He said he goes biking here and they have a great museum. I noticed the sign about a fair out front, but it's mid-September and the sign says August."

He raised an eyebrow and shook his head. "That you notice? I feel like it's there year-round."

I followed him through the parking lot and around the fence to the opening. We looked down a hill of dry grass. Zigzagged red and brown paths of dirt wound their way down the hill.

I laughed. "This is what you wanted to show me?"

"Yes," he said as he started walking down the hill. I followed close behind, careful not to misstep and go tumbling down the hill. The path went off to the left, and we followed the winding trail a way through the trees, then stopped to stare at the most breathtaking lookout over the crystal clear turquoise water.

Only one word escaped my mouth, "Wow."

The water looked almost translucent. It was intense and sparkling, inviting and exotic, so full of life. Absolutely breathtaking.

A wide variety of spruce, poplar, jack pine, and birch trees surrounded us and ran all the way around the rocky red cliffs. From fiery red to vibrant orange, yellow, red, and green, the trees stood proudly in full bloom and seemed to shimmer in the sunlight. Although I'd seen leaves change in the fall my whole life, this was different. The magic of nature at its peak.

Tim stared at the amazing view with a sparkle in his eyes. The way he stared at the nature around us with so much passion made me smile.

He grinned. "Who knew a mine dump could be so beautiful, right?"

"The water is so intense, like a tropical lagoon. It's really quite breathtaking. But why is the dirt so red?"

"It's an iron ore pit. Did you see the pit on the side of the highway on your way into Hibbing?"

I nodded.

"That one is currently being mined by HibTac, but this one is for recreation only. People come from all over to bike and hike here," he said, a proud tone in his voice. "Like Troy."

"Do you come here a lot?"

He nodded. "Sometimes I bike out here with friends or with my friend Kari and the Redhead Redfeet group. They hike the trails often. We have a lot of fun, and I'm always meeting new people. Our last hike was a little over four miles. It's a hell of a workout, and the view isn't too bad either."

Hiking intrigued me. I loved the beauty of the forests in Minnesota, the light rustling of leaves, the excitement of wildlife all around and coming upon random streams or lakes you weren't expecting, especially up north. Pure solace and a heck of a workout. I'd forgotten how much I loved the outdoors and a view like this I had yet to experience.

He sat down next to the ledge, his legs dangling off the edge of the cliff, and grabbed my hand to gently guide me down next to him. I did so without hesitation. I felt safe when I was close to him.

I looked behind us down the path. "Do you think any mountain bikers are going to race up here and run us over?"

"Nah. They can see us and if they come this close to the edge, they are the ones with the problem. So tell me something about you I don't know."

I leaned back on my hands. "What do you want to know?"

"What's your favorite holiday?"

I picked a piece of grass and tossed it at him. It fluttered and blew away in the wind. "That's an easy one. Christmas."

"Why Christmas?"

I stared over the water. "Because it reminds me of good times growing up, sitting by the fireplace in my grandma's basement with eggnog."

He stuck his finger down his throat and pretended to gag. "Gross."

"And how old are you?"

"Sorry, I just hate eggnog. It's so thick and, well... egg-like. Keep going."

"Have you ever tried eggnog? Most people who don't like it admit they haven't tried it. It tastes like a thick vanilla shake, but better."

He rubbed his chin. "I highly doubt it tastes like ice cream, but continue."

"Ha! You've never had it," I said, pointing my finger in his face.

He swiped at it, clearly exposed for his misleading behavior.

"Fine, I haven't tried it but just the look of it makes me want to gag. It's made with raw eggs."

"If they are chilled right, they aren't going to breed bacteria and hurt you."

"So you say. It still sounds disgusting. You will never get me to try it."

I laughed. "Sounds like a challenge. You just wait. I'll make you drink it on Christmas. You'll like it so much you'll have to look at me and say, Lizzy, you're right and I'm wrong. I'm sorry I ever questioned you. Eggnog is so delicious, after all."

He shook his head and poked his fingers into his eyes.

Our eyes met, and we moved closer. The kiss was so tender, I lifted my hand to his jaw to pull him in harder.

We jolted apart at a loud noise behind us and jumped to our feet.

Two women rounded the corner laughing. One cried out and put her hand over her chest when she saw us. "I thought you were some kind of predator," she said, laughing as she tried to catch her breath.

The other woman stared at us. Her eyebrows shot up with recognition. "Tim?"

I looked back at Tim. He was turned away, as if to hide his face. Their eyes met, and he fidgeted. "Hi Beth."

The woman's friend stood up straight, finally catching her breath and looked at Tim, then to me, then back at her friend."

"Wait, this is Tim?" She tensed, her nose wrinkled with a look of disgust.

Beautiful Beth, with the long dark hair and olive skin, crossed her hands and wrinkled her forehead.

She seemed to be waiting for an explanation from Tim. Like, why was he there with me? That bastard. Was this his girlfriend?

"This is Lizzy," he said, as if that explained everything.

I stuck my hand out to shake hers in apology, but neither of them responded or moved at all, so I took a step back and put my arm down.

Awkward. What was going on here?

Beth finally took a step forward and slapped Tim across the face.

I stood there with my mouth open, watching in disbelief. Did that really just happen? Was he cheating on her with me?

"You bastard," she said, jerking her hands to her hips. "I thought you were out at the lake today cleaning the boat and putting it in storage."

His shoulders caved in. "I was."

"You're so full of crap, you know that?" She turned her attention to me with a look of disgust. "Have fun with him, blondie. He's a loser. Let's go," she said to her friend.

They walked away. But not without Beth glaring at Tim and me both over her shoulder.

Obviously, she was too upset to continue on her walk since she headed back the same direction she came from.

We stood there in silence until I finally said, "What was that all about?"

When he did not answer immediately, I said, "Never mind. I don't want to know. Can you just take me home?"

"Let me explain."

He moved toward me, and I stepped back. "Please, just take me home. The moment is lost. I thought you were different."

My eyes burned, but I held back. No way would I let him see me cry.

I turned and started walking up the hill .

"Lizzy, wait! Let me explain," he said.

He chased after me until the gravel stirred up behind me and I heard a loud grunt... I turned to see Tim laying on the trail.

He stood up slowly, bouncing on one foot. I was not rushing to his side. He was probably faking it. There was nothing I hated more than a lying, cheating man. Although, Tim was so convincing he probably would have stolen my heart if we had not run into his girlfriend. Too bad for him, he was caught red-handed.

He stood up straight, and blood ran down his leg. Tears shone in his eyes and he winced in pain when he tried to walk. Damn it. I really wanted to hate him right now, but instead I ran to his side and called 9-1-1.

Chapter Twelve

Victoria

MY PLAN TO see the doctor by myself was foiled by my sister-in-law, Lyndsey. She insisted on coming with me. I'm pretty sure Troy put her up to it.

We were staying in Rochester one night, then the next night we'd get a hotel by the Mall of America to celebrate being in remission. At least that's what I told her.

I hardly slept all night at the hotel before my appointment. I tossed and turned until Lyndsey finally turned on the light and we watched *Pretty Woman* and vegged until the sun came up.

It took a lot of convincing, but I finally got her to agree to wait at the coffee shop down the street while I had my tests.

I was diagnosed with Triple-Negative Breast Cancer over a year ago. It is the most aggressive type of breast cancer, but I only told people I had breast cancer and kept the details to a minimum. With this type of cancer, I had a five-year survival rate, but I tried to play it down with Troy. He was already so concerned. My cancer was spreading, that I knew, but the real question was whether radiation or another round of chemo would somehow cure it.

Miracles happened and without hope, what did I have?

When the scans were done, and my doctor updated me, it really hit me. This was for real, and I was far from a miracle.

I walked into the coffee shop to find Lyndsey sitting in the corner, chewing her nails. She jumped to her feet when she saw me walk in. She studied my expression for a moment before she ran up to me and held me tight.

I felt a gush of tears, but I was not about to break down in the middle of the coffee shop.

"Let's take a walk, okay?" I whispered.

Lyndsey grabbed her purse and coffee off the table and followed me out the door. She put her hand on my lower back to guide me, but knew enough to wait until I was ready to talk.

We walked until I saw a picnic table and we both sat down. She laid her head on my shoulder and wrapped her body around my arm.

"This is the best hospital in the world and yet they couldn't stop the cancer from metastasizing." I turned to Lyndsey. "Lyndz, I can't believe I'm actually admitting this, but I'm going to die. It's inevitable."

Her body shook, and she cried. "Don't say that." She tried to hold in the tears, but she was as scared as me.. "We're all going to die eventually, but it isn't your time yet. It isn't your time." She repeated it as if reality would change if she kept saying it.

I turned my head away from her, unable to look at her without crying again. I wanted to keep it together. My prognosis did not seem real. I knew the odds weren't good, but I never wanted to admit it to myself. Now it was real.

"The truth is, I knew it was in my lymph nodes, but now it's everywhere. Stage four." I stared at a couple walking by. The dad had a little girl on his shoulders.

I nodded in their direction, and Lyndsey followed my gaze. "I'll never have that. I'll never get to be a mom. I never knew I wanted that until right now."

"No way. You aren't throwing in the towel. We'll fight this. You will be a mother someday if you want. You can always adopt," she said. Her voice pleaded with me, as if I had some control over the matter.

She wasn't getting it. I was going to die. I didn't have enough time left to be a mother.

I looked at her. "Lyndsey, the treatment is over. I want to enjoy my last weeks or months without spending them in the hospital fighting a battle I can no longer win." I inhaled sharply. "I want to be with you, my family, our friends. I don't want to sleep and vomit and be sick all the time. I just want to go home."

My eyes dropped to my boney wrist. My body was foreign to me. I had no fat left. My eyes were sunken in, my ribs were showing, and my hip bones stuck out. I looked like a skeleton. Like I was already half in the grave.

I did not feel good or pretty. I felt disgusting and weak. I missed having a little extra fat on my body. I never thought I'd feel that way, but I was healthy back then. I wanted that life back, but I would never have it again. I was going to leave Troy all alone.

"You have to fight. You have to," Lyndsey begged me amid more tears. "Let's call Troy. You'll see. Everything is going to be okay."

How was I going to tell Troy? Or Lizzy?

When I did not move, she took my phone off the picnic table and I put my hand on top of hers to stop her. "No."

"No?" She looked at me like I was crazy. "Victoria, you have to tell your husband."

I shook my head. "I'm not telling him, and you aren't either. Not until I have a plan."

Lyndsey frowned. "What are you talking about? A plan?"

What was I talking about? I was not sure, but I was the one who always made a plan.

Troy would not know what to do without me. It wasn't fair. I needed to make sure he would be okay. I needed to find someone to take care of him before I told him. I needed to do something, and this was the only thing I could control right now. I needed to find him a replacement wife.

I had an idea, but Lyndsey would take some convincing. "Have you ever made a dating profile?"

Her eyes widened. "What are you talking about?"

I grabbed my phone and started searching for dating apps. "I need to find him a wife."

"A wife? I think you're in shock. Do you know what you're saying right now?"

"I know what I'm saying. I need to find him a wife," I said. "If I can find someone to step in and take my place when I'm gone, he will be okay. Please, just support me. I need this."

"I think you've gone mad, but I'm here to help in any way I can. If it makes you feel better, then I'm your girl." She wiped away her tears and sat up a little straighter.

I smiled. "Thank you. Now start googling."

We spent the next couple of hours setting up a profile for Troy. I had to crop myself out of a photo from our wedding for his profile picture. Doing so was a little weird, but it was my favorite photo of him. I loved how his hair was gelled, and his blue eyes glowed with the bright blue lake in the background.

"We sure had the most amazing wedding, didn't we?"

Lyndsey gave me a closed lip smile. "The best. Everyone in Side Lake still talks about your wedding. It made Side Lake come alive even more. The idea of the whole wedding party coming in from the water on jet skis with you in the boat. It took Side Lake weddings to a whole new level."

I stared off into the passing cars. "It sure did. I want to explore the Cities for Troy's perfect match. There just aren't enough people up north, and I don't want anyone to recognize him and think he's cheating on me." The whole idea made me laugh. Troy was not that type of guy. He'd never cheat on me. He was as honorable as ever and that was why I had to do this, or he would be alone in our big house forever. I would not let that happen all because of my genetics and weak body.

Finished with his profile, I looked over at Lyndsey. "I have another idea."

She winced. "I'm scared to ask what this idea is."

"Looks like there's a grief support group in Minneapolis. Let's go."

She dug her palms into her eyes. "A what? You can't be serious. Please don't tell me this is about finding Troy a wife."

"What better place to meet a grieving widow who wants to meet a sexy, grieving man?"

"You realize you're still alive, right? Troy doesn't even know, which makes it pretty hard for him to grieve. I know you're going through a lot, but this seems kind of crazy."

She paused, clearly struggling with all this. I put my hand on her shoulder. "Why is it wrong? I'm doing this for Troy."

"You know, since you're still alive," she said with a sigh.

"Okay, but they don't know that," I said. "So it will not hurt anyone."

She followed me down the sidewalk to her car in the parking lot..

"I'm pretty sure they'll figure it out."

"Please, just let me do this. I need to do something to keep myself distracted, and although I hate to imagine Troy ever being with another woman, it's taking my mind off things."

She shook her head and got in the car.

Lyndsey shook her head. "Here we go."

The hospital was huge, but after a little direction from the information desk, Lyndsey followed me into the conference room where folding chairs were set up in a big circle. They were half filled, mainly with women ranging from their twenties to maybe their seventies.

I grabbed a chair and Lyndsey sat next to me, nervously biting on her nails.

"Calm down," I whispered and laughed softly. I busied myself with evaluating every woman in the room for Troy's type. What was his type, exactly?

"What are you going to say? What if they ask me questions? Do you want me to pretend to be a widow, too?" She put her head in her hands. "I'm so going to hell. This is crazy, you know that, right?"

I pried her hands off her eyes. "Calm down, okay? You're just here to support me. I'll do all the talking. You sit still and keep your panic to yourself, okay?"

Lyndsey nodded, but her expression showed she wanted to be anywhere else but here. She was acting like we were smuggling holy water from a church or something.

More women filled in the empty chairs around the circle, and they had to bring out three more chairs to accommodate the number of people in the room.

A beautiful woman in her thirties wearing a black pencil skirt and a baby blue button up blouse sat directly across from me. She held a clip-board in her lap and a pen in her hand.

"Hello everyone, I'm Dr. Orlando but you can call me Danny. Short for Danielle. We are all here for one reason." She paused to smile at us. "To find a spark of light in the darkness of our broken hearts." She smiled again or maybe still. It was hard to tell. I couldn't help but stare at her perfect teeth that had me wondering if they were her real teeth. They were too straight and two white. Maybe she had braces?

My mind was all over the place. What the hell was I doing here?

"Although my story is a little different than most of you, I also have had my fair share of loss, like you. I was married at the age of twenty-two and by the age of twenty-five I was a widow."

I gasped and covered my mouth. She looked in my direction and shot me a friendly smile, making eye contact with me.

"My husband died in a car accident on his way to an emergency surgery. Yes, he was also a doctor. At that time, I was a nurse, and I immediately went back to medical school and became a doctor. I knew it would keep me busy enough so I wouldn't have time to think about him, and it sure did."

We all laughed lightly. Everyone nodded with understanding.

I hated to think Troy was going to be broken like the women around me.

Hurting and all alone.

Would he ever find his happiness again? I had to make sure.

"I've done my fair share of grief counseling in groups just like this one. Last year I decided it was time to take over and facilitate because it still hurts, and this keeps me from making my job my life. I don't think the pain ever really goes away, it just hurts a little less. There is no place I'd rather be than here with all of you." She looked around the circle. "Anyone else want to share? This is a judgement free zone."

She was too young to be ten years a widow. My heart broke for her. What did he look like? Was she dating now? Would she ever have kids?

An older woman waved from her chair.

"Hi, I'm Anna. I'm sixty-five years old and my husband died last year. Next week will be the one-year anniversary of his passing, and I feel so numb at the thought. I don't think I'll ever move on. He was seventy when he died of a heart attack, and everyone keeps saying he lived a good, fulfilling life. I wasn't ready for him to leave me yet. We made so many plans for our retirement years together. We worked our whole lives and now here I am, retired and alone." She sobbed into a tissue and blew her nose lightly.

Danny smiled gently, her eyes softening. "We're here for you, Anna. Thank you for sharing with us. Do you have a good support network outside our group?"

She shook her head. "I know it isn't easy for my kids, but they have their own families to support them. I'm all alone in my big house. I want to sell it but they won't let me. They say that's where they were born and it would erase a part of their childhood. Talk about the pressure."

"Maybe one of them wants to buy your home," the woman to my right said.

"Yeah, you need to do what's best for you," I said. "If it means that much to them, they can buy it."

Anna looked at the doctor. "I should wait until the one-year anniversary before I make big decisions. Isn't that what they say?"

"At least. Have you felt this way for a while? Are you sure it's what you want?"

"Yes. My husband and I talked about this before he died. The house is just too much to keep up. I want a small apartment, but my children want to continue to come to our house for the holidays. It's big enough so my kids can all stay there with their families. I'm tired and I don't want to host the holidays anymore."

"This is your life, and you need to do what's best for you," I said, patting her arm. It felt so good to comfort someone else. To be a part of helping them during the hardest time in their life. Those who are gone have it easier than those left behind.

I knew at that moment I was doing the right thing by keeping this secret for a little while. I did not want Troy to be in pain without me. I wanted him to move on, and that was what I needed to accomplish before I left. I needed to be less selfish and find him a new wife, so he didn't have to. It would fix everything. Even if the thought of it hurt so bad I could hardly breathe. I needed to be his hero and save him from the pain of losing me.

The next hour was beautiful and made the small things in my life seem so unimportant after listening to everything these ladies had been through. How lonely and broken they all were.

Troy and I sometimes had sleepless night where we ended up screaming at each other and sleeping in separate rooms. It was stupid and childish. We would not make up right away because neither of us was willing to admit we were wrong. What was that? Why were we so stubborn? Life was short, and I was going to live what was left of mine to the fullest.

I was on a mission, and that was to find Troy a wife. I did not care what it took. I would make sure he was taken care of no matter how much it hurt.

Chapter Thirteen

Lizzy

I STOOD by his side to watch as the nurse practitioner put twelve stitches in his leg when all I wanted to do was leave him to fend for himself.

What was I doing? I was being too nice. That was always my problem. I was a people pleaser most of my life, a habit so hard to break.

The nurse stitched him up so carefully. This was what I wanted to do and who I wanted to be. A nurse. An RN. Helping people through some of the hardest times in their life. I wanted to be the person that made them feel better, that comforting voice that was soothing and calming amidst a crisis.

I no longer wanted to be the dumb girl sitting in the chair holding the hand of some guy, jerking her around and seeing other people behind her back.

I'd rather be the one stitching him up as he winced in pain. He deserved it.

I finally saw his true colors and my instincts were right about him. He was just so convincing, but I should have known better.

Once the nurse left the room, I looked at him and said, "I'm not sure what your motive is, but I'll tell you one thing, buddy. I am not the kind of girl you play. I'm the girl you bring home to meet your parents. I have more class then to settle for some douche bag womanizer, so save me the time and stop trying to convince me otherwise. I want you to take me home." I looked at his leg and realized that may be a little difficult for him at the moment. "Or better yet, give me your keys. I'll drive."

He did not argue as he handed over his keys.

We drove home in silence until we hit the turnoff to Greenrock Road and he decided it was the time to start justifying his actions.

"Beth was the girlfriend I told you about. The one who broke my heart," he said.

My scowl softened, and I relaxed a bit, but I was still angry. "That still gives you no excuse to play her."

"I didn't play her. She—"

"Just stop talking," I said, cutting him off. "I don't want to hear any more of your excuses. You guys are all the same."

"I'm sorry, and I understand if you don't want to talk to me anymore." He no longer looked like a confident ladies' man. He looked vulnerable.

"First Lisa at the restaurant and now Beth. You really had me fooled. I don't believe a word you say. Lisa hated you for a reason, and I highly doubt it had anything to do with Maddy."

"She faked cancer," he said.

"Faked cancer?" I repeated. "You just don't stop, do you?"

He stared out the window, a look of defeat on his face.

I pulled up in his driveway and shut off the car and watched him get out.

"Are you sure you don't want to take my car? I feel so bad that I couldn't at least drive you home."

"It's fine," I snapped. "It's not like my aunt's house is far."

I was angry and frozen in place. I stayed in my seat until he opened up my door, took my hand, and led me out.

For some reason, I let him. And the limp just made it that much more satisfying. He did it to himself.

I walked him up to his door. He turned to face me and took both my hands in his. He kissed me on the forehead. "I'm really sorry," he said. "I never wanted to hurt you."

He opened up his door, and I closed it behind him without saying a word.

Victoria came home in a great mood. She was glowing, and danced around the kitchen.

Her news must be good.

"Welcome back, Aunt Victoria. How did it go?" I held my breath, waiting to hear the words come out of her mouth before I started celebrating with her.

Troy came into the room before she could answer and spun her around by the shoulders. She squealed as he picked her up and wrapped her thin legs around his waist and kissed her.

The moment was uncomfortable for me, but also very sweet. I hated men, but Troy was different. I was relieved we had good news.

"What's the word, baby? I was going to call you, but I figured it would be better to celebrate in person."

He had been pacing around the last few days, hardly saying a word. He was definitely worried about her more than he let on.

The room got silent as we waited for her to answer. She tapped Troy on the shoulders, and he put her down.

"I'm sorry to say, but I'm going to be around for a while," she said with a grin that lit up the entire room.

I hugged her, and Troy clapped and kissed her.

"I knew it!" I said.

"Okay, call the gang. We're going to Valentini's to celebrate." He grabbed her and kissed her over and over, small, quick pecks, and he gave her another squeeze before walking away.

She winced in pain. "Okay, babe. You know you're stronger than you think. A little lighter, please."

"I'm sorry, I'm just so excited. I knew everything would be okay. If not, I would have fought harder to come with you. I hope you and Lyndsey had fun. What a reason to celebrate. Against all odds."

"Yep."

"What did you guys do while you were there? Any celebrating?" he said.

She waved him off. "Not really. We did some shopping. Now call Kevin and Ethan. I'll call Maddy."

"Deal," he said, and he kissed her one last time before flashing her a giant smile and pulling his phone out of his pocket as he left the room.

Victoria's face dropped after he left. She put both hands on the counter and started taking deep breaths.

"Are you okay?"

She jumped and turned toward me quickly. "Lizzy, I didn't realize you were still here. I'm fine. Just a little tired. It's been a long couple of days. Will you let Troy know I'm going to lie down for a couple minutes before we leave? I'm so exhausted."

"Yeah, no problem. Go lie down. I'll do up these dishes."

"I appreciate it."

Victoria and Troy's good news was so exciting that I forgot to think about how I would feel if Tim showed up until we got there. This was not about me, this was about them, and I was not letting my confused, lovesick brain impede the night.

I had the gnocchis. They were the best gnocchis I'd ever had in my life. I tried one of Victoria's cheese raviolis at her insistence. It was by far the best raviolis I've ever had, too. It was tender, the tomato sauce bursting with sweetness, every bite a celebration for my exploding taste buds.

Everyone was talking about how great the food was and Victoria was struggling to eat, so she made me take a few more bites to keep everyone from noticing she was not eating. I complied, but my stomach was soon swollen and I regretted it.

Lyndsey was quiet and hardly talked throughout dinner. What was wrong? Why was she so disheartened after finding out Victoria was in remission? It didn't make sense. Something else was going on with her.

But Troy stood up and distracted me. With his wineglass in hand, he said, "I want to say what great friends you are and how grateful we are to have you in our lives. We moved back here after getting some tough news." He paused and smiled at his wife. "You guys were here with open arms to help us when we weren't sure what our future held. We were scared as hell." Tears welled in his eyes. "You have no idea how much it has meant to us that you stood by us through all of this. Thank you. Here is to Victoria, and to all of you." He raised his glass and took a drink.

Victoria flashed a closed lip smile and grabbed his arm. "Sit down, Troy. Come on, you're embarrassing me."

She looked at the surrounding tables, but everyone was busy having their own conversations to notice what was going on in our corner.

Troy sat down and lifted his glass again. "Here's to friends that come together when times are tough."

"Yes, thank you guys," my aunt said, a bit bashful.

Something seemed off about her. I was probably reading too into it.

Everyone picked up their side conversations again.

I turned to Victoria. "I guess this means you'll call my mom and tell her?"

Although my mother and I did not see eye to eye, I loved her, and I knew she would be heartbroken if Aunt Victoria did not tell her.

"Yes. Maybe around Thanksgiving I'll make it down to see them. But for now, I was thinking we should plan a big Christmas celebration. We'll find the biggest pine tree and decorate it together and go on a hayride and have eggnog and bake Christmas cookies, the complete package."

Everyone heard her excitement and joined in.

"I think that's a great idea," Whitney said. "I'm in. Maybe we could even have a hot tub party and go skating at the rec center, too."

Victoria squealed and this time, people at other tables turned around to see what all the commotion was about.

"Yes! Let me know if you're here for Christmas this year. It will be so much fun."

Lyndsey cleared her throat. "Are you sure you'll be strong enough for all that?"

That was rude. Did she not like Christmas?

"Yes, I'll be just fine by then. I'll be without chemo at that point for months. I may even have a belly on me."

We all laughed with her even though her frail frame concerned me.

"For how much fun Christmas will be, we should still probably discuss Halloween first. The fall festival is coming up rather quickly. Who is volunteering this year?" Whitney asked.

Brad nodded. "Maddy and I will probably be busy enjoying trick or treating with David once it starts, but we'll be there volunteering until then."

"And if they need cupcakes, count me in," Maddy said.

"That would be great. I'm in charge of the bean bag game this year, so if anyone wants to paint a giant pumpkin, just let me know. I'm painting the ghost," Kat said.

"I'll paint the pumpkin," I said. I loved painting.

Kat smiled. "Awesome. It's a lot for me to do all on my own. Thanks, Lizzy."

"Yeah, but who carved it?" Ethan asked.

Kat punched him in the shoulder and he held it like she hurt him. "Hey," he said playfully and rubbed it.

She pouted and squished his cheeks together. "Poor baby."

Kevin cleared his throat. "Talking about carving pumpkins, where is Tim tonight?"

"He said he had some papers to grade and wouldn't be able to make it, but he'd catch up with us tomorrow. I know he volunteered to sing and play the guitar," Victoria said.

"No way," Whitney said. "His voice is amazing. I can't wait. And I know Ed is planning on bringing his horses up for a sleigh ride."

"It's going to be perfect," Victoria said. "Absolutely perfect."

Yes, perfect, but I had a major task ahead of me before I decided whether I was going to stay in Side Lake. I had to return to the Cities and make sure I was not making a mistake. I needed to end things with Dalton once and for all and tell Ava I was moving up north and going back to school. None of it would be easy. I also needed to see my mother. Life was too short to keep going on this way, and she was too stubborn to be the one to apologize first.

Adulting sucked.

Chapter Fourteen

Victoria

"YOU REALLY AREN'T GOING to tell them?"

"Not yet."

Lyndsey built a bonfire out back and told Kevin she wanted some time with me, so here we were sitting by the fire. Our winter jackets kept the wind off the lake from freezing us to the core. She was not happy with my decision, but I was not making this decision for anyone but myself. She needed to be okay with that right now.

"Why?"

She was trying so hard to convince me to come clean, but I would not budge. Not yet. I had a plan. Kind of.

"Because I don't want them pushing me to get more treatment that will keep me alive a little longer, but at what cost? I want to enjoy my friends in my last weeks or months on this earth without being in pain or in a hospital bed. Please, grant me this one wish."

She crossed her arms and pouted. She was angry she couldn't get through to me. Couldn't get me to change my mind.

"I know it isn't easy for you to keep this from our friends, from Kevin. I want you to know I really appreciate it, and I really appreciate you. This is my one wish. Just give me some time. I'll tell them eventually, I promise. Just let them be happier a bit longer."

She grunted. "Sure, use your dying wish to make me keep the biggest secret of my life."

I put my hand on hers. "Please, Lynz. Please do this for me? It's not your secret anyway, it's mine. You know I would do it for you."

She threw up her arms in defeat. "Fine."

I got up and sat on her lap and put my arms around her neck. I kissed her cheek.

She grunted. "You sure have a boney butt, you know that?"

"You love me," I said, with no plans of getting off her lap anytime soon.

I did not want her to ever forget me. I cherished our friendship so much and although I had not known her very long, she was always there for me. We bonded immediately, and she just got me.

I'd seen Lyndsey a few times back when I was dating Brad when we were teenagers, before he ever dated Maddy, but we did not know each other very well. She was much younger than Brad and me. Younger siblings were more of an annoyance, so Brad seldom took her along when we were out on the lake.

My heart hurt to know this time next year I probably would not be here to joke with her and make her keep my secrets. The thought of her forgetting me one day made my eyes tear up. "Promise you'll never forget me."

She grabbed my face. "I will never forget you, Victoria. You will live forever if I have anything to do with it."

I laughed through my tears. "That's a bit morbid.'

She laughed, too, and squeezed me.

"But seriously, I'm not going anywhere, anytime soon," I said. "I want to process this so I can be there for Troy. He was so excited when I told him the cancer was gone. He knew the odds weren't in my favor, and he wanted to believe it was true. He's not ready yet, and I need your help."

She rested her head on my shoulder. "Fine. I'm scared to ask what you need now."

"I need to find him the perfect woman and then I will tell him, promise. I don't want to have to worry about him. Please help me, I can't do it without you. I've given this a lot of thought, and it would make me happy. Please."

She shook her head. "You've got to be kidding me. This again?"

"I need you to start by taking over his dating profile. Make some small talk with a few women and find five who you think seem worthy and stalk them. Check their social media, google them, find out where they work and who they've dated. Do whatever you need to do to find the top two women, and I'll take it from there. I'll be doing the same."

She covered her eyes with her hands. "I'll do this, but remember me saying I absolutely hate this. I have a feeling this is going to backfire on me."

"Don't worry about that." I laid my head back on her shoulder. "Let me handle it. Just make sure they aren't prettier than me."

"Prettier than you? Impossible."

I was not kidding Lyndsey about a new wife. I wanted Troy to find someone, or he was bound to be alone forever. I logged into his social media and searched through all the women on his list of friends while he slept beside me, snoring loud enough to wake the neighbors. This was the first time his snoring did not bother me. I would not be hearing his annoying snore forever.

How much longer would it be? Would I really want to know if I could? Probably not. But I had to make it to Christmas. I would definitely make it to Christmas. I'd make sure of it.

Christmas was my very favorite day of the year. Ever since I was a child, Christmas was magical to me. I loved the decorations and hanging up our stockings, the smell of cookies in the oven, and the taste of frosting as I snuck a lick off the spoon when I was supposed to be stirring.

I came across the name Danny Orlando, and I clicked on her profile. What were the odds? The doctor from Minneapolis was friends with my husband on social media. I had to find a way to ask him who she was. Maybe he knew her husband who had passed away? Time to find out.

Troy was lying on the couch watching the Vikings. He'd been so much happier since he thought my cancer was gone. He knew the cancer could come back, but he was not thinking about that right now. He was believing what he wanted to believe and who was I to ruin that? I hated that I was the reason for his anxiety and unhappiness this past year.

In a way, I felt carefree. He no longer looked at me with as much concern and worry in his eyes. Like I was a fragile piece of China. We were both freer somehow.

I lifted his legs and sat under them on the couch. "Who's winning?"

"The Vikings, of course. They'll be undefeated this year, just you wait."

I almost believed him. But the Vikings always found a way to lose when it was the most important game, be it the Superbowl or the play-offs. They continued to break my heart every year since I was a child.

I rolled my eyes. "Isn't that what you say every year?"

"This is the year. You wait and see."

"Mm hmm," I mumbled.

He jumped up and pinned me beneath him. "You best be nice. You'll be eating your words. If you can't love them when they lose, you aren't a true Vikings fan, Mrs. Finney."

He held me with one hand and tickled me with the other. I kicked and squealed, laughing until I thought I was going to wet my pants.

"Stop! Stop!" I said, still laughing.

"Or what? Admit it. The Vikings are going to win this year. They are going to win the Superbowl."

"Fine, fine, they are going to win, okay? You happy?" I cried out in defeat and he stopped tickling me.

I got my knee free and rolled off the couch. He came right with me.

"Feisty one today," he said, back to tickle my boney ribs.

I felt good today, stronger. Not close to my normal self, but better. He was letting me squirm out of his grip, but it felt so good not to be treated delicate for once.

I struggled against him until he released his grip and kissed me. We rolled around on the floor, and I giggled. We were back to joking and playing around without the heaviness of cancer on his mind. We used to do this all the time until everything turned so serious. Maybe we'd actually be able to make love again without him worrying about breaking me.

Another dying wish.

He stared into my eyes, and it gave me goosebumps. "You're so beautiful, you know that?"

"It must be these sexy black eyes from lack of sleep," I said. "Maybe I should go as Uncle Fester for Halloween."

"Stop doing that. You're so beautiful inside and out. Have I told you lately how madly in love I am with you?"

I tapped my chin. "Remind me."

He kissed me again, and I squealed. I did not want this moment to end.

He stopped, and we both sat up on the couch again. My back hurt a little from rolling around, but I would not spoil the moment or he'd comfort me and apologize.

He took a deep breath and stood up.

"So, there is something I want to ask you about."

"Okay, I might have another minute until the Vikings get another touchdown. What's up?"

"I came across your friends' list on social media when I was bored."

This caught his attention. "Oh?"

"And I came across the name Danny Orlando. She looked familiar. Just wondering how you know her."

"Did something happen that I don't know about?"

I shook my head. "I was just curious, that's all."

"Her father was a doctor at the same hospital as my parents in Duluth, and they would send us both off to camp each year. She was my best friend when I was growing up."

"Did you guys date?"

He shrugged. "Nah. It wasn't like that. She was just my friend. We lost touch after my father passed away. My mother told her family about the abuse a few weeks after his death and that was it. They never talked again. I was in college at the time, and I think Danny and I were just so busy we never really kept up since our parents were no longer friends."

"Do you think she believed what your dad did?"

He shook his head. "I'm not sure. I never really gave it much thought. I know we're friends on social media, but we kind of lost touch, I guess."

"Looks like she's a doctor now."

"Good for her," he said, not a bit of interest in his voice. "She always wanted to go to med school. I'm glad she followed through. Now get over here and cuddle with me."

I snuggled in close and rested my head on his hard chest. He was so perfect. Too bad this was another dead-end road.

"Why were you snooping through my friends list, again?"

"Ah, no reason," I answered, kissing his chest.

Luckily, right at that moment, the Vikings made an interception and Troy forgot to ask me any more questions because he was too busy screaming at the television, cheering on his favorite player.

Next thing I knew, the guy who made the interception ran in for a touchdown, and the Vikings won another game.

Chapter Fifteen

Lizzy

THE SOUND of them laughing and playing in the living room set my chest on fire, which slowly spread to the rest of my body. I should not be angry and annoyed at their happiness, but didn't they know not everyone wanted to hear them get all kissy and flirty? Men sucked.

In the morning, Victoria was taking me shopping, and I planned on applying for jobs in the afternoon. I was still nervous about going back to the Cities to see Dalton. I also worried about how much trouble Dalton was in after losing all those drugs.

He was mentally abusive to me and made me feel so small, but I was still wrong to leave him to face all the people he owed money to when the drugs were stolen. Our drugs. I never tried to stop him. It was easy money.

Here I was upset about Tim and acting like my relationship with Dalton had never happened. Technically, we had not broken up. I just left. I did not owe him an explanation, but I had to for myself. I needed closure, and I needed to see that he was okay. I was not a monster like him. I was a good person.

Victoria took me shopping in downtown Hibbing as promised. We went to Moxie's, and I bought the cutest long red dress and black cardigan, along with gold hoops and a sweatshirt. The store was decorated in a festive fall theme. Antique chairs were nailed to the wall as displays for the clothes that hung from the chairs. The store was simple, cute, and so creative.

"Victoria, is that you? How are you doing?" the sales associate said.

"Great. I love what you did with the store for fall. My niece Lizzy here is up visiting me from the Cities and she's looking for a couple sweaters and a pair of jeans. Do you have any cute new inventory you think would look good on her?"

The woman eyed me up and down. "Hi, Lizzy. I think I have just the sweater for your cute figure." She ran to the back of the store behind the curtain and came out with the cutest white sweater.

"This is perfect. I absolutely love it. It looks so cozy."

"We just got it in and I thought it would look perfect for you. I haven't even had a chance to put it out on the floor yet. Want to try it on?" She pointed at the open curtain and I excused myself to try it on.

I came out, and both my aunt and the worker complemented the fit.

I tried on two more sweaters and a pair of jeans. Everything fit me just right with the woman's help. I even found a button up blouse that would be perfect for a job interview. I just needed to find a pair of black pants.

"Since you're new to the area, have you been to Benders? I think these jeans and a pair of brown boots from Benders would really give you that northern Minnesota vibe. I saw them today when I was walking by, right in the window. You should check them out."

The sales associate made me feel as though I'd known her forever. I loved how everyone seemed to know everyone in a small town. Growing up in a big city always made me feel so lonely. So many people, yet everyone was in their own world. They did not take the time to care about their neighbors. Not like up here anyway.

As Victoria paid, I thanked her, and although I knew she had a lot of money, I still felt bad for making her pay for my stuff. I was an adult, and I should be able to afford my own clothes. I needed a job.

"How about we go to Blueberry Fields next? It's this cute little boutique just down Howard Street," Victoria said after we bought the super cute boots from Benders. The associate was right. They were perfect with my new outfit.

"Are you sure? You've bought me so much already."

She waved me off and took out her keys. "I'm your aunt. When was the last time I got to spoil you? Plus, we need to support the local businesses or we won't have anywhere to shop. And you'll need a cell phone, too."

Blueberry Fields Boutique was a family-owned store with the cutest clothes. I had a hard time choosing, but eventually found a cute orange, pink, and black shake hoodie. It was trendy and fashionable, but also nice and warm. I found two pairs of jeans and a camouflage long sleeve shirt to add to my stack, at Victoria's insistance.

Troy and Kevin were having beers in the living room when we walked in.

"We were discussing the fall festival," Troy said to Victoria.

Victoria grinned. "Mmm Hmm. And what exactly have you accomplished?"

Kevin looked at Troy. "Yeah, what have we accomplished exactly?"

Troy gut punched him lightly and Kevin hammed it up and acted like he was in pain. "Whose side are you on, anyway?"

Lyndsey opened the sliding glass door and came in from outside. "How did shopping go?"

Victoria held up the bags she had in her hands and I did the same. "It went great," Victoria said.

"Show me everything."

The next few weeks were spent planning and getting decorations ready for the fall festival. The committee was full of Side Lake locals who loved getting together and planning fun celebrations in town for all the seasons.

I was in charge of painting a wooden cutout of a pumpkin for a kids' beanbag game. The project kept my mind busy and helped me avoid Tim, who also seemed to be avoiding me.

Aunt Victoria insisted on getting me a cell phone, and I accepted, but only because I needed a number if I was going to get a job. I liked not having a phone, but I also knew it was time to reach out to Ava. She helped me so much, and I promised I'd be in touch. I told myself I'd call her in November, after the fall festival was over. Maybe I'd visit her before I made definite plans about whether to go to school.

Fall Festival day finally arrived. Maddy and Brad had costumes for all of us. Maddy loved Halloween and had saved all their costumes throughout the years.

Victoria and I went to her house the morning of the festival to pick one out, but found Maddy on the floor in tears when we walked in.

Victoria knelt beside her and cradled her head. "What's wrong?"

She sobbed. "I miss Ariel."

Victoria had told me about Maddy's little girl who died in a car accident. My heart hurt at the thought. She was just five or so.

"Sorry, I have these days sometimes when I don't expect them," she said, still sobbing. "I opened up this bag full of costumes and found this cute little cat costume she wore when she was two. It was such a great Halloween that year." She held up the costume to show us.

"So cute," Victoria said. "I bet she looked adorable."

"She did," Maddy said. "And she meowed like a kitty. It was so adorable. I miss her so much."

She laughed through the tears.

I wanted to say something to comfort her, but I was not sure what to say. I knew her, but not well enough for this. The house felt claustrophobic and uncomfortable for me.

"I'll let the two of you chat." I struggled to breathe and needed to get away.

I walked outside and sat down on the step in front of Maddy's door. A few minutes later, Victoria came out and sat next to me.

"You don't need to come after me. I'm fine. Be with Maddy," I said.

She wrapped her arm around my back. "You've been through so much, Lizzy. It's okay if Ariel made you think of your dad."

"It isn't fair. I hate that he left me with my mother. I know it sounds terrible, because his death was out of his control, but if he were still alive, my mom would still be my mom."

She embraced me in a tight hug, not letting me go. "I'm so sorry. I didn't realize you felt that way. What happened to your mom is terrible, but it isn't your fault or your dad's fault. She doesn't like to deal with anything, so she numbs the pain. I wish things could be different for you. I'm so sorry I wasn't around more after the accident."

I shook my head. "I wasn't your responsibility. You were such a great aunt, and I always knew I was safe with you. My mom was just this grenade, and I never knew when she would explode. Seeing Maddy grieving brought back so many emotions from my past that I never dealt with. My mom, Dalton, my dad."

Maddy peeked her head out the door. "Okay guys, the waterfall has finally dried up. Who is ready to try on costumes?"

"Be right in," Victoria said with a friendly smile.

"Take your time. No rush at all," Maddy said.

By her expression, she knew something was going on with us. Hopefully, she did not think it had anything to do with her.

"Are you okay? We can go home and I'll grab the costumes quick and meet you in the car if you want."

I shook my head. "No, I'm okay. I get first dibs, though."

She smiled. "Of course you do."

We stood up, and she hugged me again. "I'm so glad you called me. I want you to know that. It means so much that I was someone you could call when you needed help."

I was so glad I did, too.

Chapter Sixteen

Victoria

THE SIDE LAKE Fall Festival began, but seeing Lizzy so broken was heavy on my heart as I stood behind the counter, refilling the plates. We had hot dogs, chips, fruit snacks, popcorn balls, and pumpkin bars thanks to one of the longtime Side Lake women who planned most of the event.

I loved how the community came together to put on an event full of laughter and fun for the whole family.

The guys were in charge of the bonfires, to make sure they kept burning and to help the kids with their s'mores when their parents weren't close by. Tim was playing the guitar and singing, as promised. Most of the crowd sat in chairs in front of him and ate the delicious food while they enjoyed his music.

I looked over at Lizzy. She was standing in front of the pumpkin game, her eyes on Tim. She would hand a kid the bean bags, stand behind the pumpkin, then glance over at him. I was not sure what happened between the two of them, but the way they looked at each other meant the attraction was still there.

Lyndsey came up behind me. "Need any help?"

I nodded toward Tim. "Why do Lizzy and Tim keep looking at each other when they think the other isn't looking, yet they avoid each other at all costs?"

She shrugged and grabbed an apple out of the bag for the bob for apples game and took a loud, crunchy bite. "Hmm. I'm not sure, but they're so obvious. Maybe they got into a fight or something. Maddy probably knows. She talks to Tim all the time." She looked around. "Oh, there's Brad. Let me grab him."

Before I could protest and tell her she was making a big deal of this, she came back with his arm in her grip.

"What's all this sexual tension between Lizzy and Tim? We need to know," Lyndsey said.

Brad would tell us bluntly. He struggled to hold back and glanced at Tim. "All I know is they were out on a date and they ran into Tim's ex and it didn't end so well. That's where the sexual tension comes in."

We stared at them until Lizzy turned her head and caught us. Busted.

"I think he's just giving her space." Brad shrugged, then grabbed a bag of chips. "They're both playing hard to get, if you ask me."

"I hate to admit it, but I think he's right. It makes sense," Maddy said. "I have to run some marshmallows over to the bonfires. They're going fast. So many kids want plain marshmallows. Can you believe that?"

I shrugged. "Not me. I love chocolate too much."

"Me too," Lyndsey said.

I looked at my watch, then back to the dirt road that led up the hill to the rec center building. I was just about to check my messages when she finally showed up.

Troy's future wife was wearing the cutest Chestnut Chicks Mukluks with white fur and a silver button. Her jeans were tight and showed off her slender body. She had on a black hat and a thick red and black flannel jacket with a black scarf wrapped around her neck. Her blonde hair hung in loose curls and she had on bright red lipstick.

She walked down the hill with her own cup of hot chocolate or possibly coffee in a Stanley mug. I knew everything about her. She was thirty-five years old and had no children. If my research was correct after stalking her social media, she loved kids. She just hadn't met the right person to have them with.

I found her on social media, and we bonded over books. She was born and raised in Ely and still lived there. She owned her own apparel business.

Ely was focused on the outdoors and apparel and rentals for the boundary waters. It's a beautiful tourist destination in the summers, but the winter was a little quieter. Like Side Lake and most of the northern cities of Minnesota, Ely was geared around the outdoors. Just the kind of woman I could see Troy falling in love with.

Everything she wore said rural woods and the outdoors. Troy loved hunting and fishing and being in nature and I did too, but since I'd been so sick and weak, I no longer did those things. Just that one day I pushed myself to kayak with Lizzie.

I took two steps in her direction before Lyndsey grabbed my arm to stop me. "Is that Jessica? Please tell me you didn't invite her here, Victoria."

"It's fine. I want to get to know her. It's not like I'm setting her up with my husband right now or anything. I'm just getting to know her in person. I got her a great deal at Kat's bed-and-breakfast she couldn't turn down." I turned to Lyndsey and bent the arm she was holding. "Please, trust me."

"You are going to hurt him. Just tell him the truth about your cancer, please. This isn't healthy."

I moved my arm out of her grasp. "I will. I promise. I just need a little more time. Now please come and meet my new friend. It's harmless, I promise."

I knew how seeking this woman would seem to Lyndsey, but I really liked her. Maybe she was not a match for my husband in the future, but she was a great distraction and another friend I could bond with over books.

I ran up to Jessica and hugged her tight. "Jess, it's so great to meet you. I want to introduce you to my sister-in-law, Lyndsey."

Instead of shaking her hand, Lyndsey gave her a hug. "So great to meet you, too. Victoria told me all about you. I think we may need to start a book club because between you, Victoria, and Kat, I'm feeling like a slacker. I want to get back into reading."

Her welcoming conversation with Jess warmed my heart and eased my nerves. This was her way of showing her support and letting me know she was here for me. She was letting me grieve and supporting me in all my crazy ways. I loved my friend.

"I would love to be a part of your book club," Jessica said. "I'm in one in Ely, but we read a lot of literary fiction. I'd love to read more fun books like romance or thrillers."

Lyndsey looked at me. "Did you tell her about Ethan?"

Jess frowned. "Ethan?"

"Oh, Ethan. That's for another day. I don't want to scare her off yet."

We both laughed.

"Have some food, Jess. We'll all be getting together after the festival is over and then you can meet everyone."

"Sounds great. Is the woman who owns the bed-and-breakfast here today? Or can I go there and unpack?"

"I'll send you the address. Feel free to head over there. Her daughter Emma is there to help you check in. I'll text you when we're done and let you know where to meet us."

"Sounds like a plan. Great meeting you," she said as she waved goodbye before she walked away.

Once she was out of earshot, Lyndsey looked at me and said, "You have until Thanksgiving. I'll help you do whatever you need to do, but then you need to tell everyone."

"Deal."

Thanksgiving was longer than I expected she'd let me have. I had a lot to do to prepare and a lot to do before everyone started questioning my health and giving me constant looks of pity. I was going to make the best of the time I had left for being normal in their eyes.

Lyndsey grabbed onto my arm. "You don't look so good. Are you doing okay?"

I looked down at my shaky hands. "I need to sit down for a minute. I'm going to try to eat something."

"I'm here if you need anything."

I was weak and exhausted. I needed to eat something, but I wasn't hungry. I grabbed a bag of chips to force myself to eat and sat down in front of Tim. How was he not famous yet? He sounded so good, I couldn't help but sit and stare, along with everyone else.

Chapter Seventeen

Lizzy

I WATCHED his beautiful ex-girlfriend as she walked up to Tim with lovesick eyes. The more I tried to stop looking, the more my eyes were drawn to them. Beth and Tim. Tim and Beth. The thought made me ill.

This was the moment of truth. I would be able to tell how he felt about Beth by the way he looked at her. She sat on a hay bale in front of him with her beautiful long brown hair blowing in the wind.

The moment he realized who it was, his eyes jerked my way. He smiled nervously. I did not smile back. What did his smile mean? He never tried to contact me once since our run-in with Beth, and he had stayed away from any of the gatherings with our friends.

I wanted to give him the benefit of the doubt, and maybe I should have let him explain that day, but what if he was lying? What if he was just like Dalton?

Dalton was great at first. He was outgoing and outspoken. He made me feel like he would protect me from everything in the world. Then I realized he loved to be mean and hated the world. He would say horrible things and beat me down with his remarks once we moved in together. He started speaking for me and dictating what I could and could not wear, when I could or could not leave the house. He stopped allowing me to wear makeup and made me feel as though I was trying too hard if I dressed nice.

I fought him at first, but then I became so tired of fighting that it was just easier to do what he wanted. Pretty soon, obeying Dalton became my life. I did not know how to get out of the trap, and I was scared to leave. I was afraid of what he would do if I left.

Not everything was bad. I missed going to movies together and the days he made a big sale and we'd go out to dinner and celebrate and talk about buying our own house someday. He was there to listen when I was upset about my mom and her drinking.

He would yell at me and break me down, but later on he would apologize and sometimes he would even cry. He grew up with parents that did not get along. His mother never let him spend time with his father, and he resented her for it. He told me he struggled with trusting women. She would not let him join sports because she did not want him to get hurt. He wanted nothing to do with her once he got old enough to make that choice.

I know he loved me, and I know he wanted to do better, but he was so mean sometimes and all he wanted to do was play video games and grow marijuana in our basement. The memory angered me, but I needed to know that he was okay. I needed to make sure the criminals had not returned to rob him or something worse. I still cared about him.

I went into the bathroom and texted Ava.

Me: Hey B, it's Lizzy. I made it to Side Lake safe and sound.

I watched as the three dots appeared.

Ava: OMG! I've been so worried about you. Are you okay?

Me: I'm doing good. I'm thinking about coming down for a visit...

I was not second thoughts, but I needed to figure this all out. I needed to make sure I was making the right call.

Ava: Are you sure you are ready to come back? Dalton has been really weird since you left. Nick says he is okay, and I know they are brothers, but he's over here all the time. It's weird.

Me: Is Dalton still selling?

Ava: I'm not sure. Where are you going to stay? I would let you crash here, but I don't think Nick would keep it a secret from him.

Me: I think I'll stay with my grandparents. It's just for a few days. Is Dalton pissed at me?

Ava: Do you really care? Look what he has done to you. It's not OK.

Me: I need to make amends. I'm not planning on coming back for good, but I really want to see you.

Ava: I would love to see you! When are you planning on coming? Soon?

Me: Yes, I'll text you. Sometime this week. Don't tell him I'm coming though, okay?

Ava: Yay! I got you. Gotta go. See you soon B!

Maybe an unexpected visit was the best thing for Dalton. How would I get there? Would Victoria let me use her car? It was worth a try. How was I going to bring this up and when? Should I stay with Ava or my grandparents?

Cleanup went smoothly. Everyone worked together and when it was all done, we were exhausted, but not too exhausted for Bulldogs at Riverside.

The bar was pretty quiet, with all the summer people long gone.

I rode over with Victoria, and when we got there, she headed straight to the bathroom. She looked exhausted and weak, and seemed to be geting worse, not better. I hoped she would start doing better soon. I was worried about her.

I found a table and moved over more tables to make room for everyone. I spotted Tim walking over from my peripheral vision.

"Let me help," he said. He picked up the other end of the table and moved it with me.

"Thanks," I said with little enthusiasm.

I sat down and he sat down next to me. He took off his hat and set it on the table. "Listen, I want to apologize."

My anger made me belligerent. "For what?"

I wanted him to tell me what he did wrong. Was he the man I thought he was, or was he just another player?

"I'm sorry I didn't call you to explain further. I'm sorry that I let you down. And I'm even more sorry that I hurt you."

The bartender sat down with six Colorado Bulldogs and menus before walking away. Victoria must have ordered the drinks on her way to the bathroom or the bartender was a mind reader.

Tim waited for me to respond, but I stayed silent.

He sighed. "I really like you, Lizzy, and I was hoping you would let me explain."

I looked away. "Not here."

"How about if I take you out for breakfast tomorrow? I know an amazing bakery where I'd like to take you. It has the best pastry and coffee around. What do you think?"

"I think you're trying to bribe me." I crossed my arms.

He slouched, no longer his confident self. It pulled at my heart-strings.

"I am, but so we can have some time alone and I want to show you around. I promise you're going to fall in love with their cinnamon rolls."

"Fine, but that doesn't mean I'm forgiving you." I took a sip of my drink, then punched the hazelnuts off the top of my drink and ate them both.

"Sorry I took so long. I ran into one of our neighbors from down the road," Victoria said when she joined us. She looked at Tim, then back at me. "Should I come back?"

Before I could tell her not to go, Lyndsey, Kevin, Kat, and Ethan walked in and sat down.

Kat looked at the drinks on the table and then up at Victoria. "Are the rest of the clan not coming?"

She shook her head. "Maddy and Brad were taking David home and Whitney and Josh were exhausted and wanted to go home early with Brittany, so it's just the six of us tonight."

"What a night! I can't believe how many kids and families showed up tonight despite how cold it was." Kat rubbed her arms as if remembering the chill of the night. "Burr."

"And you blew everyone away with your singing, Tim. Wow, absolutely unbelievable. Thank you so much for volunteering," Victoria said.

His smile widened. "I had a great time today, and the kids had so much fun. Although I'm with Kat on how cold it was. My fingers are still numb."

"Did you guys see the little girl dressed in the Bluey costume? She was definitely warm enough with those cute little paw gloves and that hat. So adorable," Victoria said.

Her expression turned to worry as soon as she said it. I was not sure why, but she was worrying me. Something was wrong. Maybe she was unable to have kids after the chemo. That had to be it.

"Don't forget Whitney's daughter in her Ariel costume. I thought that was such a beautiful tribute to Maddy's daughter," Kat said.

"I know it made Maddy and Brad's day. They never want her to be forgotten," Victoria said.

"That's so beautiful." I took another gulp of my drink. "They seem like great people."

"They are," Victoria said. "And they're your friends now, too. You're family to them. We're all family."

A woman walked in the door. "Ah, here she comes," Victoria said. She ran over to greet the woman and led her toward the table after stopping at the bar to order another Bulldog.

"Everyone, I want you to meet my friend Jess. She's staying at Ethan and Kat's B&B for the week."

Everyone shook hands with her, except Lyndsey. She just nodded and smiled at her.

"I checked into your place, Kat. Wow, it's so beautiful overlooking the lake."

Kat and Ethan smiled at each other. "I'm so glad you like it. Any friend of Victoria is a friend of ours," Ethan said.

"I'm not going to lie," Jess said. "I know you wanted to keep it a surprise but after Victoria talked up this Ethan, I had to look him up and I cannot believe I'm standing in front of the one and only Elizabeth Conrad."

Ethan blushed, and Kat put her head on his shoulder. "He's taken," she said with a laugh.

Jess laughed. "I knew you lived in Minnesota, but I had no idea you lived in Side Lake. It's so great to meet you. I love your books! I blame you for the fact that I'm still single. Your stories have a way of making me believe in love, and I can't settle until I find the right one. If there is the right one out there for me."

Everyone nodded.

"You guys must think I'm stupid."

Victoria stepped in. "Not at all. It's just that we all found the love of our lives. We understand more than you know."

She smiled. "I love that. Maybe it will rub off on me."

"You never know," Victoria said with a twinkle in her eye. "Anything can happen."

Chapter Eighteen

Victoria

I'M NOT sure when Beth got there, but she came in by herself and sat right on Tim's lap. He looked quite uncomfortable, and Lizzy looked broken. Beth was flirty but also madly in love with Tim. She kept touching his stomach. He got up minutes after she sat down and went to the bathroom.

When he came out of the bathroom, he sat at the bar. I excused myself and joined him while everyone at the table was deep in conversation. "Hey," I said to him and then ordered another drink. "Why are you sitting way over here?"

He was leaning over the bar more than sitting comfortably on the stool.

He put his fingers in his hair and stared down at his drink. "I've found myself in an unpleasant situation, and I'm not sure how to solve it."

"Try me." I sat up straight and took a sip of my drink. I had told the bartender to serve me pop with a little cream and hazelnuts on top because I could no longer handle alcohol or I'd get sick.

"As you know, Beth is my ex. I found out she was cheating on me with a friend of mine, so we broke up and then he cheated on her. Go figure. She called me crying, and I agreed to be friends but—"

I cut him off. "But you can't just be friends, and she wants to get back together now that the other guy rejected her."

His eyes opened wide in surprise. "Exactly. How did you know?"

"Because it's obvious."

He looked confused. "It is?"

I took a drink. "Listen, do you still love Beth?"

He tapped the side of his glass, deep in thought.

His silence was answer enough. "You don't need to tell me. But you need to decide before Lizzy gets too attached. You're a single guy, so I get it, but you need to make your choice and make it fast." I stood to leave, but he said my name and I turned around to look at him.

"I'll make this right, I promise. I really like Lizzy a lot."

I could see it in his eyes. He was a good person, and I trusted him.

"I know," I said.

Not long after I left him at the bar, he came over and said good night to everyone.

Beth frowned. "You're leaving already? Me too. I can give you a ride."

He shook his head and glanced at Lizzy, who had left her chair and was headed to the restroom as soon as she saw him come over to the table.

"You really shouldn't drive after you've been drinking," Kevin said. "Let her give you a ride home."

Tim nodded, but he did not look happy about it. I had a feeling this would be the moment he made his choice, and we would all see her car in his driveway if he decided on Beth.

If he chose Beth, Lizzy would be hurt, but she would get over it, eventually. That was better than him being in love with someone else when he was with her.

Lizzy came out of the bathroom and looked at all of us sitting at the table. "Aunt Victoria, will you come outside and get some fresh air with me?"

I followed her outside.

"I was thinking about going back to the Cities and tying up some loose ends."

She looked more at her hands than me while she was speaking.

"Okay. How are you getting there?"

She looked away. "Well, that was what I wanted to ask you. Do you think I could use your car? I'll only be gone a few days."

I thought about it for a moment. "You aren't running from Tim, are you?"

"Not at all. He's making his own decisions. I will not let a guy I hardly know get to me. But I left so suddenly that I need to go back and see a few people. Tie up some loose ends. Make sure Dalton knows it's over."

"Do you want me to come with you?"

She shook her head. "No, no. You stay here. I'll only be gone a couple of days. You can say no. I don't mind taking the bus."

"No, take my car. I insist. Take your time. I'm in no rush to get my car back. I want you to do what you need to do. If you change your mind, I'd love to go with you."

She hugged me. "I know, and I really appreciate that."

"When are you leaving?"

"Is tomorrow too soon?"

I heard the door open and close before sun rise though the sun would not appear until close to eight o'clock. I got up, and the coffee was still hot. There was a note taped to the counter right in front of the coffee maker.

Aunt Victoria,

Thank you so much for letting me take your car. It means so much to me. Thank you for continuing to open up your home for me until I find a place.It really means the world. Thank you for being there for me. I don't know what I'd do without you.

Love,

Lizzy

This simple letter brought tears to my eyes. We'd lost touch for too long and now she was back in my life and I hated that I would be breaking her heart again when I told her my secret. Watching Maddy cry over missing her daughter had upset Lizzy so much because she struggled with losing her father and pretty much her mother at such a young age.

I would tell all my friends over Thanksgiving dinner and then I would drive down to the Cities and tell my parents and Diane. My confession was going to be brutal. I was just glad I had time before I had to face that.

While Lizzy was gone, I kept my mind busy by searching for that perfect person for my husband. Maybe I had already found her. Maybe it was Jess.

I drank my morning coffee and read two chapters in my Abby Jimenez book, then made my way over to Kat's B&B on my snowmobile. The B&B was just a couple of doors down, but I thought it would be a great day to snowmobile, partly because I was feeling good.

I opened the door and found Kat, Ethan, little Brittany and Jess sitting at the table eating breakfast.

"Well, good morning. I thought it would be a great day for some snowmobiling. Jess, what do you think? We can ride up to the Viking and have some burgers for lunch."

Jess took a sip of her drink before attempting to speak. "That sounds like a lot of fun. I'm in."

"Great." I looked over at Brittany. "And how is Miss Brittany this morning? You got to have a slumber party with Auntie Kat last night. Didn't you?"

She nodded. "And Auntie Kat says if I eat real good, she's gonna take me sledding and ice skating at the rec center today."

"That sounds like fun. Where's your mom and dad today?"

"They're doing some Christmas shopping in Duluth, so they asked me to watch her," Kat said. "They're also getting a turkey for Thanksgiving, so we don't have to. I told we'd cook it if she buys it."

"I loved our turkey last year. It was just so moist and it melted in my mouth," I said.

Ethan cleared his throat. "Well, I'm picking up Kevin and Troy and heading into town for our hunting licenses and a few things we need for the shack next weekend." He dumped the rest of his coffee in the sink and kissed Kat.

Jess looked at Ethan curiously.

"Is it opening weekend already?"

"Yep," Kat said. She turned to Ethan and rubbed his scruffy face. "And it's no shave November. Is Troy doing this, too?"

I laughed. "Yep. It's the one month each year I don't get on him for not shaving. They have to keep warm in the deer stand."

"You know you love it," Ethan said. "I never knew what I was missing when I lived in New York. Maybe I should submit my next author picture with this beard. You think anyone would recognize me?"

"Since you've only been growing it two days now? Yes, I'm pretty sure they would."

We all laughed, and he waved before taking off.

"Well, if you guys want to meet us at the hill after your snowmobiling, we'll be there most of the day sledding and skating. Miss Brittany here even brought her ice skates. I'll have to dig mine out of the basement."

"I didn't bring mine," Jessica said. "But I'm not really a fan of ice skating anyway, so they're probably rusty."

Strike one. Troy loved skating with me in the winter. He liked to play hockey on Thursday nights at the rink at the rec center. Did she like to watch hockey? Would she be supportive of his hobbies?

I tried another tact. She had to be a hunter. "How do you feel about hunting?"

"Well, I'm not a big fan. The truth is, I'd rather just stay inside and read all day. I had a boyfriend once who liked to hunt, but I wouldn't step foot in his house because he had guns. I don't see why he needed a gun in his house."

"Oh. But you live in Ely and you own an outfitter store there," I said, confused.

"It's actually my parents' store. I still love outdoorsy clothes, but I'm not a big fan of hunting and fishing and all that outdoors stuff."

Strike two and three. She was definitely not the girl for Troy.

Time to start from scratch. This was becoming a full-time job.

Chapter Nineteen

Lizzy

THE CITIES HAD HARDLY any snow when I arrived. I sat in bumper to bumper traffic and realized how much I had not missed the traffic. I loved the outdoor feeling of Side Lake and the lack of busy people. No one was in a rush at the lake. It was so relaxing and peaceful. There was never any traffic.

The 'Welcome to Burnsville' sign came up and my heart bounced off my ribs with anxiety. I pulled up in front of our duplex and the vision of being held at gunpoint by the druggies played in my head. My hands shook on the steering wheel, and I struggled to take off my seatbelt.

It took me more than five minutes, but I finally made it to the front door. I took a deep breath and knocked.

I knocked and knocked again until finally I heard some movement inside. I stepped back on the steps to leave room for Dalton to open the door.

And he did.

I gazed at his handsome face as he opened the door.

"Lizzy?" he said, as if he did not recognize me. "Why are you here?"

Some things never changed. I felt less guilty as my heart sank at his words.

"You think you can just come back here and everything is going to be okay?"

"Well... that's not why I'm here."

He leaned out the door to look around in what seemed a paranoid gesture.

"Come inside." He pulled me in the front door, then shut the door and locked all three locks like a crazy person.

I eyed him suspiciously. "Is everything okay?"

His eyebrows drew together, and his nostrils flared. "Really, Lizzy? Were you not right there with me when those two pieces of shit held us at gunpoint?" His voice rose. "But I sure as hell was the only one to return home while you slutted your way around town."

"It's not like that Dalton" I pulled on his arm. "I was scared. I don't want to be a part of your drug trade anymore."

A dark laugh escaped his lips, but I could not look into his eyes. They were scary and frightening. Nothing like I'd ever seen him before.

"Funny, you sure didn't mind the money, though, did you?"

"That's not fair, Dalton! We had no choice. I'm not judging you. I just can't do it anymore. You need to understand." My nerves mixed with my guilt had me begging for his forgiveness.

"Understand what? You only care about yourself. Why are you even here, anyway?"

I needed to get out of there. I no longer wanted his forgiveness. This was a mistake even coming here.

"Listen, Dalton, I wanted to stop by to tell you I'm sorry and that you and I both know it never works out between us. We want different things."

He deadpanned. "You found someone else, didn't you?"

I shook my head.

"I can see it in your eyes," he said as he stepped forward. "I can keep you safe now. I got a gun just in case they come back."

He did not know how to shoot a gun. He was not a hunter, and he'd never owned a gun before. The thought of a gun in Dalton's hands terrified me.

"Okay, I got three guns," he said. "Wanna see?"

He headed for the kitchen. I ran up behind him and grabbed his shoulder to stop him. "No, please don't get the guns. I don't want to see them," I said, a sense of panic in my voice.

"I want you to see that you're safe now. I'll take care of you. I have one in the drawer by the front door. I also have one in the closet next to the back door, and I have one under my pillow, just in case."

"Under your pillow? Wait, they aren't locked up?" The thought made me want to get out of there as fast as I could.

"How would I get to the guns quickly if they showed up again and the guns were locked up and not loaded?"

I shook away the thought of a loaded gun under his pillow while he slept.

"Dalton, a loaded gun under your pillow could go off . That scares me."

"It's just a little pistol. It's no big deal. It has a safety on it. It's fine and perfectly safe."

He could be so convincing, even when I knew he was out of his mind. I reached out and held his arms, but it was a gesture to hold myself up more than intimacy. "It is a big deal, Dalton. You're sleeping with a gun under your pillow. Have you called the police?"

"Are you stupid? And tell them what, exactly? That I was selling drugs? That they robbed me and stole thousands of dollars in drugs? Are you stupid?'

"I've had enough, Dalton. We are over. I'm leaving." I turned around and headed for the door.

"There is another guy! I can't believe it. I was right," he said. "Am I not enough for you?"

Before I could move or say anything, he pushed me up against the wall and pinned my neck with his forearm. His arm pushed so hard against my throat, it was hard to breathe.

The hot air from his mouth blew in my face. I tried to turn my head to the side to avoid what I could while trying to pull his arm and relieve the pressure on my neck. "Stop...it...you're...hurting...me." I said, gasping for air with each breath.

The front door swung open, and Nick and Ava came in. Nick saw what was going on and rushed to pull him off me. "What the hell, Dalton? What are you doing to her? Are you stupid?"

He threw Dalton to the floor and sat on his chest when he tried to grab me again.

I was hysterical and sobbed hunched over on the floor, trying to catch my breath. Ava got down on all fours next to me. Once she saw I was okay she put her face next to mine, and her hand rubbed my back.

"You need to go, Lizzy," she whispered. "You need to go now. I don't know how long Nick is can hold him."

I nodded and coughed. I sat up and she helped me to my feet. No way was this real. Was it really happening?

"You can't drive like this," Ava said, her lips pursed together. "I'll give you a ride. C'mon, let's go."

"No, how will you get—"

"There's no time, she said, pulling me outside. "I'll drive your car. We need to get out of here. Who knows what he'll do next?"

I knew she was right. I had to get out before he got ahold of me again.

As we pulled away from the curb, I saw two guys pull up and get out of the black Soudan.

I pointed behind us. "That's them, Ava. That's the guys."

She kept driving. "What guys?"

"The guys!"

The car screeched to a halt when she finally understood what I was saying. She left the car right there in the middle of the road in park and took off running toward the front door of my old duplex.

I screamed and cried after her. "Ava! Ava come back! They're dangerous!"

She kept running, so I decided it was time. I called 9-1-1.

I pulled my car over to the side of the road and waited until the sirens got closer. I watched as both police cars pulled up and got out of their cars in a mad dash for the front door of Dalton's house.

I held my breath and prayed my best friend would not come out in handcuffs.

Dalton was escorted out the front door in cuffs.

He shouted at me when I got out of the car. "This is all your fault. She did this. The drugs are hers. That bitch set me up!"

The police officer made no move toward me as they stuffed him into the back seat of the squad car.

"Tell it to the Judge," the police officer said.

I stared down the road long after the police were gone. That could have been me.

Two more squads pulled up.

"Do you live here?" one police officer said as he made his way up the sidewalk.

I shook my head.

"How do you know the guy who lives here?"

"He was an old friend," I said, my voice shaky.

Two police officers walked out of the house with Nick and Ava in cuffs.

I ran toward them. "They're innocent," I said. "I'm the one who called. They did nothing wrong. Let them go!"

The officers kept walking Ava and Nick to the squad car and another officer walked my way.

"Miss, can I ask you some questions?"

"Am I under arrest?"

He shook his head. The two drug dealers came out next in cuffs and got into the back of another squad car.

I put my head down as the cop car they were in drove past us. The officer led me to the front yard I'd spent so many hours mowing over the summer.

"We have a search warrant. Dalton reports the two of you are in a romantic relationship and that you live here with him."

"I moved out months ago, officer. I live four hours north now. He's lying," I said, hearing panic in my voice. Did he believe me?

"I believe you," he said, as if reading my mind. "We've been watching this house for quite some time. You're lucky you got out. Most victims don't get out that easy."

Victims?

"Do you know if there are any drugs or guns in the home?" the officer said.

I nodded. "He told me there are three guns. I know he has drugs because he just admitted it to me, but I don't know where they are. He has a pistol under his pillow, and he keeps a gun by both the front and back door. That's all I know."

He jotted something down in his notebook and then looked up at me again.

"Miss, are you willing to come down to the station and answer a few more questions?"

Was he arresting me? Was I being charged with something? I was too scared to ask. Instead I said, "Sure, officer. Whatever you need."

Chapter Twenty

Victoria

WE WENT SNOWMOBILING to The Viking for burgers, as planned, and then stopped at the rec center to see my friends, but Jessica complained the whole time. Her feet hurt, she was too cold, the wind was in her eyes, and she needed a hot shower. She also forgot to mention she didn't eat red meat until we got there. By the time I dropped her off at Kat's, I vowed to never take her out into the wilderness again.

I followed her inside the B&B. "Would you like me to make you a nice warm cup of apple cider while you hop in the shower?"

"That would be really great, thank you," she said. "I don't think I'm going to shower yet, though. Would you like to come warm up by the fireplace with me?"

I walked into the living room where she was sitting on the fireplace hearth, rubbing her hands together to warm up.

"I'm sorry if I was a downer today," she said with a sad look in her eyes. "I'm much more of a stay inside and relax and read a book kind of person, but you seemed so excited."

I sat down on the recliner in front of her after handing her the coffee cup. How did I read her so wrong? "I'm sorry. I guess I assumed you loved the outdoors when I found out you were from Ely. I should have asked you more questions before I decided for you."

"It's no problem. I appreciate you inviting me out here and giving me such a great deal. I really am having a good time."

I leaned forward and clinked my mug with hers. "Let's talk books."

Her face brightened up. "Who is your very favorite author?"

"Meghan Quinn. You?"

"I'm more of a thriller reader. Frieda McFadden, Lisa Jewell, Rachel Hawkins, I could go on and on."

When we started talking books, I liked her. She became the person she really was, and she stopped pretending to be who I wanted her to be. She may not be the perfect match for my husband, but she was the perfect book friend for me.

I crawled into bed next to Troy, a William Kent Kruger book in his hand. He looked over at me and lowered his book to the bed. "How did it go today with Jessica?"

"Well, I took her snowmobiling and sledding, a day spent outdoors, and guess what?"

"Let me guess, she doesn't like the outdoors?"

I gasped. "How did you know?"

"I could tell. She didn't seem excited about snowmobiling and from talking to Ethan she seemed appalled about hunting."

"But she's from Ely!" This made no sense to me. Ely was a town of outdoors enthusiasts.

How was I the only one who did not see this coming?

"That doesn't mean she likes the outdoors, babe. She helps run her family's business. You don't have to love the outdoors to live there, although it would be hard not to, since everything is focused on the outdoors."

"It's the boundary waters. How could she live in Ely and have never gone canoeing?"

He shook his head. "You have to be kidding me. She's never gone canoeing?"

"Nope. Never."

"Not even at camp?"

I shook my head. "Never. I'm pretty sure she didn't go to camp."

"I can't say I'm surprised," he said, kissing up my arm. "But other than Jessica not liking the outdoors, how are you doing? Feeling?"

I rolled onto my side and stared into his eyes. He reached out and tucked my bangs behind my ear.

"I'm doing better."

"Relieved about your cancer?"

I was a terrible person, and I hated lying to him, but it was in his best interest. I could hide it for a while, but lying to his face when he asked me point blank was impossible.

Avoid and deflect.

"I'm so grateful for my life and my friends and this handsome man I wake up next to every morning,"

I leaned over and gave him a small kiss, but he held me there and the kiss grew deeper. My fingers were soon in his hair and his in mine. We rolled around on the bed. My body was on fire. I straddled him, both of us still fully dressed in our pajamas. I pulled my hair tie off my wrist and put my hair back. My eyes locked with his eyes the entire time.

He looked up at me, admiration in his eyes as he watched me. "Mrs. Finney, how did I get so damn lucky to call you my wife?"

I leaned over and kissed him again, pulling away and tracing his bottom lip with my finger. I would not forget this perfect face for as long as I lived. I loved every inch of his perfect body.

I sat back up and made him sit up, too, then pulled off his shirt. He wrapped his arms around me and kissed me so deep my body tingled.

And for the first time in over a year, we made love all night long, and it was by far the best sex we ever had. And just like that, our intimacy was back, and I felt justified in my reasoning to wait a little while longer before I crushed him with the truth.

. . .

It was close to noon when we finally woke up. I had three missed calls from Jessica and a text. She was heading back to Ely because her mother was ill and needed her to run the store. I wished her the best with promises of getting together soon, but in reality, I was not sure I'd ever see her again. The thought was like a force pinning me to the bed, unable to move. I might not be alive long enough to follow through with that promise, and that was my scary truth.

I felt the gentle kisses over my shoulder blades gently making their way up the back of my neck. I rolled over to meet his lips with mine.

"Good morning, beautiful."

I smiled back. A very satisfied and giddy smile. "You mean good afternoon."

He looked over me at the alarm clock. "Holy crap. I don't remember the last time we slept in this late."

"I guess that's what happens when you have a marathon of sex kind of night."

"I don't know what you're talking about, Mrs. Finney. Remind me?"

He smothered my smile with his mouth again, not letting me take a single breath, and we spent the next two hours beneath the sheets. For the first time in months, I was not thinking about dying and leaving him all alone. I let myself get lost in the moment and in his arms. I was shaky and weak and exhausted, but it didn't matter. I wanted this more than I wanted anything in so long.

Except for going to the bathroom, showering together, and throwing in a pizza, we spent the whole day in bed. We shut off our phones and snuggled. Marvin Gaye played through the speakers from the living room.

Troy sat up and our conversation turned serious. "Since things have changed a lot these last few days, I've been thinking about opening up my own business."

Guilt stabbed me sharply in the gut and I winced. A lump appeared in the back of my throat. "What kind of business?"

"What do you think of a coffee shop and bakery? We could build a little place out here and people could come in by car or by boat."

We had the investment, and this would be a way for Troy to keep his mind busy when he found out the truth. And the coffee shop was something we could do together until I no longer could.

"What about having a used bookstore, too? It would be a great way to get the women in here. We could start up a book club and maybe some authors would come in to do some book signings." I thought about Ethan being a famous author. "We could even see if Ethan would teach some writing classes. Customers could stay at Kat and Ethan's B&B. Tim could even sing!"

Troy squeezed my arms. "Slow down." He laughed and kissed the top of my head. "I think with time we can definitely make it happen. I like it, but let's start off small at first."

With time. Those words scared me. He did not know how scary they were. I had little time.

He ran his fingers through my hair and snuggled up to my back. "Are you sure you don't want to travel again?"

"No. I'm happy here. We've been all over the world. Let's stay with our family for now. With everything we've been through this last year, the one thing I know is life is short. I don't want to take the little things for granted, and although the world is beautiful, I want to be right here. With you. In this moment."

"Agreed," he whispered in my ear and kissed me.

Chapter Twenty-One

Lizzy

AN HOUR LATER, I was in an Uber on my way back to Dalton's house from the police station to pick up my car. My hands were still shaking. My timing could not have been any worse than showing up at his house. Then to see my best friend and her boyfriend arrested after protecting me. Why did Ava have to run back in there?

I pulled up at my grandparent's house. My mother's little red Camaro was parked in the driveway. People did not drive sports cars in the winter in Minnesota. They drove all wheel drive and four-wheel-drive cars, but my mother always insisted on driving in style.

The car was not in great condition, and the bumper barely hung on, but it did not bother mother at all.

The front door was open, so I walked in. Grandma was sitting in the recliner, her cane resting on the side. She brightened at the sight of me.

I hugged her. "Grandma."

"Liz-Liz. How I've missed you."

Her hands were shakier since the last time I saw her.

"Where are grandpa and my mom?"

She pushed her glasses up on her nose. "Your mom is taking your gramps to the doctor. What a wonderful surprise. You don't look very good. Are you okay?"

I kneeled down in front of her. "Not really. Dalton and I were having some issues, so I went to Side Lake to stay with Aunt Victoria and Uncle Troy. I came back to the Cities to get my things and break up with Dalton for good and when I got there he—"

"Slow down," grandma said, putting her hand on my shoulder.

I broke down and started sobbing. "It's just so bad, grandma. Dalton isn't the person I thought he was, and he was so angry, and then the police came."

"Come here," she said, her arms now open for me to hug her. As I leaned into the hug, it reminded me of the day I showed up at Aunt Victoria's house and she hugged me. This was what love felt like.

"Oh, grandma. I've missed you so much. I'm sorry I was gone so long."

She pulled out of the hug so she could look at me face to face, then she reached out and wiped my eyes.

"I am not angry with you. I'm so glad you're okay."

"My friend Ava and her boyfriend, who happens to also be Dalton's brother, came in when he was pinning me against the wall and pushed him off me. Now they're both in jail and I don't know what to do."

She smiled so calmly. "There's nothing you can do right now. If your friends need you, they know how to reach you."

I looked down at my phone. "You're right, grandma."

"Of course I am," she said with a laugh. "I've been around the block a few times. This is what grandmas are good for."

I hugged her again.

"So, you are staying in Side Lake with Victoria. It's such a beautiful place. I sure miss the lake even this time of year. Have you gone figure skating? Sledding? Oh, how I miss Bimbo's pizza, and their wings are delicious. Have you tried their wings, dear?"

She made me laugh. "I think you need to come up north for a visit. You and gramps."

She clapped. "That sounds like a wonderful idea. What have you been doing there? Working at all?"

"Not yet, but I helped set up for the fall festival and painted a pumpkin. I'm having so much fun."

"That's wonderful, dear," she said in her sweet voice.

Although she was shaky and had a bit of a stutter now when she spoke, she had not changed a bit with her old age.

"Have you spoken to your mom at all?"

I shook my head.

"Don't you forget, she's a stubborn woman like your ol' grandma. She has some big demons. She won't make it easy for you."

I nodded. "I know. Trust me."

I looked down, feeling a bit defeated. She reached over and raised my chin so I was looking right at her. "Don't let her walk away. You tell her how it is. You can do it. I know you can," she whispered.

The door opened and my mother and grandfather came in. My mother was pushing my grandfather in a wheelchair.

"Why, if it isn't sweet, little Lizzy. Come, give your grandpa a hug."

I walked over and reached down to hug him.

My mother cleared her throat. "Not even a phone call, huh? You just show up here and expect all to be forgiven?"

"Would you rather I leave?"

She did not have a reply. Instead she said, "Have you eaten? I have some tuna salad in the fridge."

"I'm not hungry, mom. I was in town, and I wanted to see you guys. I wanted you to know I've been staying with Aunt Victoria."

"My sister?"

"Yes, mom. My only Aunt Victoria."

She walked past me and pushed grandpa's wheel chair so she could get to the couch, obviously angry with my mocking.

She put her nose in the air. "I don't have a sister."

"Mom, come on. What is your problem with her?"

She put her finger in my face. "Don't you dare come in here acting like you know it all. This is my life, and she is always judging me and telling me what I should and shouldn't do."

"She's worried about you."

Grandma got to her feet and took small steps until she was right in front of my mother. Now it was her turn to stick a finger in my mother's face. "We've had enough of your drinking, girl. You've ruined every relationship in your life, and your father and I have had to sit here and watch you drink yourself to death. Your sister loves you, and she'll never give up on trying to help you get sober, so grow up, Diane! Take some responsibly for your actions."

My mother dug her palms into her eyes. "Mom, the love of my life died. What do you expect me to do? Just get over it? I need your support, not your insults."

"You spin my words," grandma said. "You've been doing it for years. You're losing your one and only daughter. Grow up and make up with your sister. This is ridiculous to watch." She threw up her hands in defeat.

My mother stood there, staring at grandma with an open mouth.

"Go ahead," my grandma said. "Apologize to your daughter for the way you've acted. She lost her father, too, you know. It's about time you start thinking about someone else for a change."

Go, grandma. Finally.

My mother turned to me with anger and tears in her eyes.

"Do you feel this way, Lizzy? I want to hear it from you."

"I do, but I love you and I don't want to fight anymore." I moved to hug her, and surprisingly, she did not pull away.

When was the last time I hugged my mother?

"As for your aunt," my mother said. "I'm not ready to forgive her. She was never here for me through any of this. When was the last time she even called me? She's too busy living that glamorous life of hers."

"Mom, you don't know what Aunt Victoria is going through. She has been back in Side Lake now for over a year. She is blogging from home, going through chemo—"

Oh no. I did not just say that. I wanted to take the words back, tell her I lied, but it was too late. I bit my lip.

"Victoria has cancer?" my grandma said. Her eyes watered. "What happened? Is she okay?"

My mother turned around to face my grandmother. "She doesn't have cancer, Mom. Lizzy just made that up. Didn't you, Lizzy?"

I stared at the floor and avoided their eyes.

"No way. You're lying. I'm calling her now" My mother picked up her phone. "How dare she keep this from us."

"No, mom! Please don't. I promised her. She was going to tell you guys. I promise she was. Please, just wait until she tells you. I didn't mean to let that slip."

She put down her phone and grandma sat back down, a look of shock in her eyes.

I hugged grandma again.

"Why didn't she tell us?" Grandma whispered in my ear, loud enough for everyone to hear.

"She found out she had cancer about a year ago, and she didn't tell anyone. I only found out because I showed up at her house and one of her friends accidentally let it slip. They didn't know I didn't know."

"Her friends?" My mother glared at me, her teeth clenched together. "She told her friends, but she didn't have the decency to tell her blood, her family?"

I shook my head. "It's not like that. They live right next to her, and they helped take her to her chemo and doctor appointments. She didn't want anyone to know until she was in remission."

Grandpa looked up and said something for the first time. "And is she in remission?"

"She is. She's going to be okay."

My grandma reached out to hold my grandpa's hand as he rolled closer to her in his wheelchair. "What kind of cancer did she have?"

"Breast cancer."

"What kind of breast cancer?" my mother said. "Breast cancer doesn't run in our family. How could she have breast cancer?

I had no idea. I just sat there, unsure of what to say.

"You don't know?" my mother said. "You must not be too close then. See, she won't let you in either."

"Stop it, Diane!" my grandma said. "You've done enough here."

"It's not like that," I said. "She cares more about me than you do."

It was true, but my words broke her.

She stared at me, speechless.

"You won't tell her I told you, will you?" I looked around at all of their faces, hoping to see signs of agreement.

Of course, my mother would tell her just to feel powerful and in control. I was used to the horrible things my mother said and did. It's why I stopped talking to her. Our relationship was toxic, and I needed to keep her at a distance if I was going to maintain any kind of relationship with her.

Grandpa wiped his eyes with a tissue. "When was she planning on telling us?"

"I think Thanksgiving. Yeah, that sounds about right."

"Then I guess we're taking a road trip to Side Lake on Thanksgiving," my mother said.

"That's a great idea," I said, with a squeak in my voice.

Did I just invite them to Thanksgiving dinner in Side Lake?

"Under one condition. If she doesn't tell us by the end of the night on Thanksgiving, I want you to know I will say something," grandma said.

"Okay, I can agree to that." Thanksgiving was more than enough time for Aunt Victoria to tell everyone. I would make sure. Now, how was I going to break it to her that I accidentally invited everyone to her house for Thanksgiving?

Surprise!

Chapter Twenty-Two

Victoria

LIZZY WAS GONE two weeks before I got a text message alerting me that she was on her way home from the Cities. She checked in a few times while she was gone to let me know she was still alive and to make sure it was still okay she had my car a little longer. I knew she would come back when she was ready, and I didn't want to rush her.

I'd spent the week planning the next steps for my mission to find Troy a wife and how I would tell everyone about my cancer on Thanksgiving. I wanted to tell everyone separately, but that might end up being too mentally draining for me.

In my heart, I wanted to put off the sad looks and goodbyes, and I wished I didn't know what was coming. I wanted it to happen quick without the prolonged dying experience of being in horrible pain. And I hated that everyone I loved would need to take care of me and that I'd end up being a burden when I could no longer take care of myself.

I wanted something to look forward to. By Thanksgiving, I would have the perfect woman picked out for my husband, and I would be ready to start planning my funeral.

Dreary. Sad. Dark. But real. And better than one of my loved one's doing it after everything I would put them through over the next few months.

Planning my own funeral was weirdly exciting. Not many people could say they got that opportunity. My funeral would be a happy affair, and people would wear bright colors and talk about me and what they loved about me, not sad and dark. Why did we think that was ever a good idea?

I had too much time to think about what happened on the other side. Was it happy and exciting? Did the deceased experience everything they did not get a chance to on Earth? Was there a higher power? Was there no such thing as time? I had so many questions. But for now I was going to focus on being alive. Carpe diem, as my old high school English teacher would say. Seize the day!

I found a cute wooden countdown to Christmas advent calendar at the Goodwill in Hibbing. It had little doors in it with a number for each day of the month where you could place a brief note or something small inside. I knew this was exactly what I needed. I planned on filling every box with notes. I would tell everyone my grand plan for the calendar on Thanksgiving, and then December first we would begin opening them together. This Christmas would be the best Christmas ever.

Lizzy came home and seemed a bit upset, but as the days ticked on, she did a little better each day. Something happened when she was in the Cities, but she never mentioned what and I did not want to push. She would tell me when she was ready. I was just glad she was not going back. I was so happy to have her here. I was not getting any stronger, and I was struggling to swallow and it was hard to hide how weak I was getting.

On the Saturday before Thanksgiving, Lizzy and I were sitting by the fire having a glass of wine when I had an idea. "I know it's not Thanksgiving yet but what do you think about doing some Christmas decorating with me?" I said. "This place looks so blah, and I think Troy would love to come home after hunting for the past week to find Christmas thrown up all over our house. What do you think? Are you up for the task?"

Last year, I decorated the day after Halloween and Troy helped. I wanted to wait this year until Lizzy came back so we cold do it together. That was the past part about putting up decorations with my parents when I was a child. Doing it as a family.

Lizzy jumped to her feet. "I love decorating for Christmas! It's never too early. Where are the decorations?"

I loved how giddy and excited she was. Maybe I'd pass all my decorations down to her, or at least what Troy did not want to keep. He loved Christmas, but I had a feeling he would not want to decorate the house for the holidays after I was gone.

Unless he met a woman and she decorated for him.

I jumped up and led the way. "Follow me. It's all under the stairs."

I had no problem carrying the bin full of Christmas decorations, but having the strength to get up the stairs with the bin was another story.

My hand shook a little as I climbed the stairs, but somehow I made it. To be able to carry the bin on my own felt so good.

"Unpack the bin while I go for more," Lizzy said.

She could tell I was struggling, but she avoided embarrassing me.

I opened the first bin to find it filled with ornaments. Lizzy's bin held my animated Santa Claus that walked up and down a ladder while Christmas music played in the background.

My mother's Christmas Village hid in the bottom of my bin. I unwrapped the first house, and I teared up. I decided at that moment I would pass the village down to Lizzy when I was gone.

"This was my mother's Christmas village. She stopped putting it out when she started struggling to walk. Your mother and I weren't allowed to touch it when we were little. Your grandmother was very strict about that, but sometimes when she was gone your grandpa would let me play with it. This village was one of my favorite parts about Christmas. ."

I arranged the village on the shelf, examining each piece as I unwrapped the tissue paper.

"I always loved this village when I was a little girl, too," Lizzy said. "I guess grandma got less strict because she let me play with it whenever I wanted."

We both laughed.

"This is my favorite piece," I said, picking up the little girl with a long blonde ponytail and earmuffs.. "I always thought she looked just like me. One time, my mom came home and caught me playing with her. She yelled so loud I dropped the little girl and broke off her earmuff." I showed her the little girl's head, and she touched the missing piece lightly.

"I always wondered what happened to her. She's so beautiful" She hesitated. "I spent a few days with grandma and grandpa at their house when I was in the Cities."

I knew she had. My mother had called to invite herself to Thanksgiving since Lizzy said I was hosting.

I was not upset. I was glad they were coming. "Yeah. How are grandma and gramps?"

"Grandpa doesn't walk at all anymore. He was racing around the house in his wheelchair. He's a hoot. And grandma was scolding him a lot. It was funny."

"And your mom?"

Her eyes widened, almost surprised I asked. "She's okay. She actually spent some time with me. We get along best if I stay away from her when she drinks."

"Did you tell her you're staying here?"

She picked at her fingernails. "Yes?"

"Why did that sound more like a question?"

"Well, I told them, but then mom said she was planning on coming here for Thanksgiving." She bit on her lip and stared up at me.

She was scared to tell me she invited them.

"Yeah, she told me."

"I'm sorry, Aunt Victoria. I really didn't mean to. It just slipped out."

Lizzy looked nervous. Almost like she was hiding something. I waved her off. "No, it's fine. I love that we'll all be together for Thanksgiving. I have more than enough room. Plus, I was planning on calling and inviting them, anyway."

She looked up at me. "Really?"

"Yes, really. They're family. When was the last time we were all together for Thanksgiving?"

Her eyes widened. "I don't know. Years."

This was going to be the best Christmas ever. Even if Diane was still drinking. I'd keep a close eye on her so she didn't get too drunk.

The tree was pretty easy to put up with Lizzy's help. She was so smart and detail oriented. She would do great things in life, I could tell. She just needed to believe in herself.

Once we strung the lights, I sat on the floor next to the bin full of ornaments because I was so exhausted, I could not stand up any longer.

"How about I take them out of the boxes, and you put them on the tree?"

She smiled. "Sounds like a plan."

I had a feeling she knew the decorating was taking a lot out of me, and I was struggling to stand. I handed her an ornament, and she hung it on the tree. "So, have you talked to Tim at all?"

"Nope."

"The morning you left, he showed up here to take you to the bakery. He seemed pretty disappointed you weren't here. He said something about how the two of you had plans that morning." I tried to read Lizzy's expression. She seemed deep in thought.

Then she laughed. Her laughter got louder and louder, an uncontrollable belly laugh. It was so contagious I started laughing until I was hunched over.

"I totally forgot we had plans. Well, he deserved it. He let Beth give him a ride home and who knows what happened between them."

"You can thank Deputy Finney for that one. He didn't want Tim drinking and driving, so he told Beth to take him home. I'm all about not driving drunk, but Beth, of all people? Tim's ex? Kevin put Tim in a tight spot. I'm sorry about that."

She shook her head. "It's not his fault. Tim never should have gone with her. He could have walked home. Anything but get in the car with her. Did you not see her sitting on his lap?"

I nodded. "Yeah. It was hard to miss."

"I'm glad I made him sweat a bit. He deserves it. I bet they're back together by now."

"I guess you'll find out soon enough, but my bet is they aren't." I winked at her.

She looked hopeful. "You don't think so?"

"Maybe you should pick up your phone and ask him."

"Maybe later," she said. "Right now I'm in a Christmas state of mind. How about some Christmas music?"

I smiled. "I thought you'd never ask. It's not Christmas without Dolly Parton and Kenny Rogers."

"Yes!"

Chapter Twenty-Three

Lizzy

IT WAS the day before Thanksgiving.

I was nervous about my mother and grandparents arriving tomorrow. What if my mother picked fights with Aunt Victoria? What if she brought up the cancer? No, she wouldn't, she promised. And she would have already let it slip if she planned to fess up. Not that they ever spoke, but she could have called and told her just to be evil.

A good foot of snow blanketed the lawn outside. The weatherman was predicting a couple more inches overnight and close to a foot on Thanksgiving.

Last year only a bit of snow fell and winter was way too warm. It didn't feel like the holidays. Now the temperature was close to ten degrees, and I was grateful for the cold, snowy winter.

I wanted to cross-country ski and skate and sled and everything else everyone did during winter at Side Lake.

Victoria had me run to the grocery store with a long list. She even ordered a second fridge for the basement. She was singing and whistling

Christmas songs as she cleaned the bedrooms and someone put up a ramp outside for gramps. She did not want moving around to be a struggle for him in his wheelchair. We both knew how much gramps wanted to be independent and do things on his own.

I still had not heard from Tim. I was about to give up on him when he showed up at my door. I was busy cracking eggs and throwing cheese and bacon and hash browns in the crock-pot for a delicious breakfast bake. The breakfast would to be ready when we woke up, when I heard the knock on the door.

I yelled, "Come in."

Tim strolled into the kitchen. I dropped the glass I was washing on the floor and it broke into a million little pieces.

His face turned red, and he dropped to his knees alongside me to pick up the glass.

"I'm so sorry I startled you. This is my fault. Let me get this. Let me," he said, crawling around on the floor.

"Don't you think you've done enough?" I said. "Why show up after all this time?"

He picked up the glass piece by piece and set them in his other hand.

"I needed some time to think."

I stopped helping with the glass and stood up. "About what, exactly? What is it you needed weeks to think about before you could show up here? Why are you punishing me?"

"I wasn't trying to, but I had to think."

"Think?" What exactly did he need to think about? "Just get out of my house. Put down the glass and leave." I clenched my teeth and pointed to the door.

"But..."

"Just go," I said. I stomped my feet, my finger still pointing at the door.

He let out a deep breath and ran his fingers through his hair. "I'm sorry, Liz. I really am."

He dumped the glass in the garbage and left.

· · ·

Watching him walk away was hard. He looked like Uncle Jesse from *Full House*. He had perfect hair, sexy dimples, and tan skin. He was so beautiful. But looks only got you so far, and I was not about to settle for someone who would treat me like I was second best. I'd been through enough with Dalton.

Tim could be really sweet and we got along well when he was not being a jerk, but the damage was done. He would not fool me. Dating had to be easier, and right now I was not looking for a relationship, anyway.

I bent down for one last piece of glass. I grabbed it the wrong way and cut myself. My finger started bleeding and Mr. Stamos walked around the corner with a damn band-aid.

"You were supposed to be gone."

He held out the band-aid. "I had a feeling you'd need this."

"How did you get in? And you expected me to cut myself, really?"

"You were so upset, I had a feeling you might try to pick up a piece of glass too fast." A glimmer of mischief spread across his face. "And I used the front door."

I let out a frustrated moan. "Fine, give me the band-aid but then you need to go. I'm not in the mood for your crap."

He gave me puppy dog eyes. "If that's what you want."

He walked toward me, and I made sure my feet were planted on the floor. I was not meeting him halfway.

He touched my wrist, and my entire arm broke out in goosebumps. I looked away so he would think it was just a coincidence. A Minnesota winter was damn cold, that was why I had goosebumps. He had no effect on me.

I watched as he opened up the band-aid, but then I made the mistake of looking into those beautiful eyes, and I could no longer pull my eyes away from him.

His eyelashes were longer than any man should have and damn, even they were gorgeous. Up close, his skin looked so soft and flawless, his lips delicious. I imagined the way my lips would feel on his.

He wrapped the band-aid around my finger, then slowly moved his hand to my cheek and cupped it. He closed in on me and my body leaned into him.

I needed his warm lips on mine. I needed to run my fingers over his muscular shoulders and through his hair.

I lost all sense of reality and control. Our lips locked, and the fire burned in my chest and my stomach, and an ache built up inside me.

Then reality hit, and I pushed him away. "This was a mistake. Just go."

A moment of weakness.

He did not fight me, nor say anything. This time he walked out the door, and I was afraid he would never come back.

By the time my family showed up, the kitchen looked spick and span. Victoria was pleasantly surprised, and she thanked me over and over. My grandparents entered, followed by my mother. She had angry eyes and a glare that did not leave her eyes. Was she already drunk?

"This house is even more beautiful than I remember," grandma said. She made her way to the kitchen table with support from her cane. My grandpa followed her, wheeling himself to a stop.

"I love what you've done with the place," my grandpa said.

"Thank you. Troy and I have been doing some remodeling. I have a lot of extra time on my hands now that I'm not traveling," Victoria said.

"And why exactly is that?" my mother said with a dark smile.

She was trying to see if she could get Aunt Victoria to break. But my mother did not know Aunt Victoria's strength. The woman beat cancer, after all.

"Well, Troy and I are starting our own business. A coffee shop and used bookstore. I'll be living my dream of having my own bookstore."

"Sounds so much better than traveling," my mother said with an annoyed roll of her eyes. My mother had her phone in her hands so she would not have to look anyone in the eye. A coward's way. I would have said it to her face, but I did not want to make her angry since she was still keeping her word about not telling my aunt the secret I accidentally let slip.

"I do miss traveling, but Troy and I would rather be closer to family and friends. We know that's what is most important and look, here you guys are. This is going to be the best Thanksgiving we've had in a long time. I'm so glad you're all here."

Her words were so genuine, and she looked happy. Not defensive at all about my mother's words. My guess was she expected this anger and rudeness from my mother. I think we all did.

"I'm so glad you could make it," Troy said, hugging grandma and grandpa and then waved at my mom. "I hate to run out of here, but the game's on if anyone wants to watch. It's a close one."

Grandpa wheeled himself toward the living room. So excited, he almost hit the lamp with his wheelchair. "I'm right behind you," he said to Troy. We all laughed. Silly old gramps.

"You look exhausted. How is everything?" my grandma said, turning her head to face Aunt Victoria.

"I'm doing okay. You know how much work it is this time of year," Victoria said.

Somehow, we made it through the night without my mother opening her big mouth, but we still had one more day to get through, and I was nervous as hell she would not keep her promise.

Chapter Twenty-Four

Victoria

MY SISTER WAS A MESS, and Lizzy seemed on edge throughout the next day. I put Lizzy to work making a pumpkin pie and a chocolate pudding pie. My sister made her favorite banana cream pie, and I cooked the sweet potatoes and made the mashed potatoes. We turned on the Christmas music and my sister only complained once before she headed for a nap.

Lizzy went to make a phone call while my mother and I did the dishes together. I washed, and she dried.

"Your sister has been cutting back on her drinking since Lizzy came to visit her," my mother said.

I nodded. "I hope she can keep it up."

"She misses you, you know."

That surprised me. I grabbed a bowl from her. "I miss her, too. I hope this can be a fresh start for us. I think it's pretty big that she came here today."

My mother touched my back. "You're different. Lighter somehow."

"Mom, I wanted to wait to tell you this, but I feel like I need to tell you now. I have cancer."

My mother shook her head as if shaking my words away.

She snapped her towel and stared at me. "Have or had?"

I cleared my throat. "Have."

She took a deep breath. "It's okay. We can fight this. Are you doing chemo or radiation?"

I took her arm and led her to the table to sit down. "No, Mom. I'm done fighting. I've been fighting it for a year now. I've done chemo, and it didn't work. I'm terminal."

Her eyes widened, and tears shone. "Terminal?" She repeated the word in disbelief.

She gasped, her body unsteady at my admission.

I held her hand. "I'm sorry I didn't tell you. I thought I could beat it but the cancer is just too aggressive. It's in my lymph nodes and my bones. It's only a matter of time."

She cried into her hands and I wished there was something I could say or do.

"It isn't right for a mother to lose her child. I always thought I'd go first." She wiped her tears away. "That's why you look at life so differently. I knew it the moment I got here. When I saw the way you looked at us."

"I haven't told Troy yet."

"What!" She shook her head. "What is wrong with you, Victoria? How could you not tell your husband? What are you waiting for?"

I looked away. "I don't want him to worry. He thought I was better, and he's been so happy. I hate to be the reason he's sad again."

"You don't want him to worry and be sad? He needs to prepare. You don't have a lot of time left. Do you?"

I shook my head. A wave of nausea washed over me.

"Months, maybe weeks. They aren't sure."

She nodded until finally she looked up at me. "When are you going to tell him?"

"At dinner tomorrow."

"I'll be by your side. Are you sure you don't want to warn him before you make the big announcement? He might feel betrayed."

That was a fear of mine, but telling him alone was even scarier. I did not want to see that look in his eyes. The look of a broken man.

"I thought about it. I'm not sure I can. I fear how he'll react. I don't want to hurt him again. We've been through this once before when I was first diagnosed. It's just so much, mom. He's going to be all alone."

She patted me on the back.

"Of course you're scared, but I don't think you're giving him enough credit. He's your person. Tell him. Let him make his own decisions."

I poured myself a glass of red wine and put on my thick winter coat and black hat so I was warm enough to stand out on the balcony behind my house and stare at the snow and ice-covered lake. The snow was beginning to fall again, and the snowflakes were giant sized. They were falling so fast I could not keep them from getting caught on my eyelashes. And it was absolutely beautiful.

I needed some time to get away from everyone and just stand on the back deck alone to think. To really appreciate the small things like the beauty in the snow.

Lyndsey snuck out and closed the door quietly. She knew I did not want to be bothered. She pulled out a pack of unopened cigarettes. "I know you haven't smoked since you were a teenager, but I thought maybe this would be a good time to remember the good old days."

I laughed. "I don't think I could take a drag without hacking up a lung, but you go ahead. Who told you I used to smoke?"

She shrugged and pulled out a lighter. "Brad, who else?"

Brad. Sometimes I forgot I dated him for a bit back when we were young. He was cute and a bit of a jerk, but wasn't that the way teenage girls liked them for some reason? The bad boy. He sure changed a lot since then.

"So tell me how you are feeling about tomorrow."

I closed my eyes and focused on the chilly breeze blowing my hair and tingling my cheeks. "I'm not ready to tell everyone, but I'm pretty sure I'll never be ready. A part of me believes I'm not terminal if I don't tell anyone." I laughed. "If that makes sense."

She took another drag of her cigarette. "It makes perfect sense. You've been through so much."

I took the cigarette out of her hand and against my better judgement, I took a deep inhale, and as expected I started coughing. I nearly vomited off the railing.

Lyndsey took the cigarette back and threw it into the snow. "Okay, that was not worth it. I'm throwing these damn things out in the garbage. Sorry, I thought it would be fun to remember the days when we were young. Be a little reckless, not hack up a lung."

I put my hand on her arm. "Thank you. It brought back some memories of my adolescent years. We sure weren't very smart back then, were we?"

"Speak for yourself. I was so cool."

I laughed and shook my head.

"Sure you were."

She turned around to go inside. Troy was on the other side of the door.

They nodded at each other in passing, and he walked out with slippers and no jacket.

"Why does it smell like cigarette smoke out here?" His voice sounded like it had a bit of an edge to it. He was not happy.

"I don't know what you're talking about. I don't smell anything," I said. I batted my eyelashes and reached for his hand in a truce.

He did not reach back. He stood there with a hard-eyed expression on his face. Pissed. He stared at me with such darkness it scared me.

"I just got a strange message on social media," he said.

Oh no. This would not be good. I waited.

"From, ironically, the same woman you asked me about the other day. You might remember. Dr. Danielle, or you may know her as Dr. Danny Orlando?"

Busted. I swallowed. "I remember her."

"She happened to run across my profile on some dating app and asked me how everything was going with my divorce."

"Shit," I said, turning around and leaning on the railing. I felt dizzy.

"She said she saw you at a grief support group in the Cities. Can you please tell me what is going on, Victoria?"

I froze.

He turned me around to face him. "I'm not sure what's been going on with you lately, but you've been off ever since you got back from Rochester. What is it you aren't telling me? Have you decided to leave me since you found out your cancer is in remission or what? Using our wedding photo and cropping yourself out pretty much explains itself." He looked disgusted, but also on the verge of tears. "Is this like some woman cancer survivors thing where you have gone temporarily insane?"

His voice got louder and louder as he spoke, and he was rambling. He was shaking and his teeth chattered.

"Oh, Troy. I'm so sorry. I was going to tell you."

"Tell me what? That you were trying to hook me up on a dating website? What the hell, Victoria? What kind of sick joke is this?"

I felt ill, and fire burned in the pit of my stomach. I needed to sit down. "Can we sit down somewhere?"

"No," he said, standing up taller. "You need to tell me what's going on. I feel like I don't know you at all."

I started crying. Hard. I wanted to tell him, but I could not get the words out.

He pulled me in and wiped my tears away gently. He held me at arm's length and looked at me. I thought he was going to shake me for how angry he looked.

"Please. Tell me. What is going on with you? Was this some kind of sick joke?" His eyes softened.

"I'm not leaving you," I said, cry-laughing. I snorted and then laughed about that.

He shook his head. "Then what is this?"

"I'm dying, Troy. The cancer is back. It's spread." I paused. "I lied to you," I whispered.

He pushed me away from him and held onto the railing. Fear consumed his angry expression, and he took deep, shuddering breaths. "Damn it, Victoria! Why wouldn't you tell me? You've known for what? A month now?"

I nodded. "I wanted you to be happy for as long as possible. I hated the way you looked at me when you knew I had cancer. I hated the way everyone looked at me. Like I was some poor, pathetic person."

"They love you. I love you. We look at you that way because we care and we want to be there for you." He turned his back on me and angrily covered his face with his hands.

"Troy, we finally had sex. Tell me you would have been turned on if you knew. You wouldn't have. You hardly touched me this past year. I want that back. I want you to be happy again. This ruined everything!"

I kept crying. I could not stop. I lost my balance, but as I fell over, I caught myself on the railing. He turned around and steadied me.

I would have rather fallen than see the look in his eyes. Pain and sadness, glossy tears and a runny nose. He was too handsome and strong to look that way. The look I feared had returned, back to stay.

"You are absolutely beautiful, Victoria. Cancer or not, I'm attracted to you. Can't you see that?" He nervously ran his hand through his hair, then looked back up at me. "Tell me you'll do chemo again. Tell me you're going to fight this, Victoria."

I hung my head.

"Victoria," he said louder, sterner. "You're going to fight this, right?"

"It's over, Troy, stage four. I want to make the most of what time I have left with you. I don't want to be sick and weak and spend my last days in the hospital. Give me these last few months, please. Be okay with my decision."

He shook me. "But the cancer will grow. It'll grow." He let go of me and shook his head in defeat. "Don't let it grow. Stay here. Stay here with me. Fight. Fight, damn it!"

He leaned forward and kissed me with his cold, wet lips. My body shook from the internal sobs, then I let out a deep cry.

My big, strong husband leaned over until his face was on my chest, and he cried. And I held him. And he cried. I cried. I ran my fingers through his hair and rubbed his head. I've never hurt so much in my life.

I broke him. He was not okay. I needed to fix this, somehow.

"You can't leave me. And you taste terrible, like cigarettes," he said, lightening the mood with a laugh.

"Please don't make me go through chemo again. Please. Just be my partner and help me live my last few months or weeks to the fullest. I need to be strong."

He shook his head again. This time he rested our foreheads together and squeezed me tight, as if for the last time. "If that's what you want, I'll support you, but it doesn't mean I like it."

"Thank you, baby. I know it's hard to understand, but I promise you, it'll be so much better. You'll see. I need this. We need this time together."

We sat in awkward silence for a moment, too long, until he said, "You made an online dating profile for me so I'd find someone else, huh?"

I nodded, unable to meet his eyes. He must think I was crazy.

"You really are a firecracker, you know that? Baby, I don't want anyone else. I only want you. Promise you'll stop setting me up, okay? There is no one in this world who could ever compare to you. You hold my heart."

"Okay," I whispered back. "I just want you to move on when I'm gone. I don't want you to be all alone."

"Baby, there's no one in this world who could ever replace you. You'll be around for a long time. I'm not letting you go."

I knew he had absolutely no control over the cancer or how long I lived, but his words made me feel better at that moment.

He won. I would pause his dating profile for now, but I would not let Lyndsey delete it. He would need it one day, and he would do a crappy job of trying to set it up without me."

Chapter Twenty-Five

Lizzy

WE HEARD Aunt Victoria and Uncle Troy fighting outside because we were all sitting by the fireplace and close to the door. We could not hear what they were saying, their voices muffled by the closed door. Lyndsey sat next to me and smelled horribly like cigarettes. I never would have guessed she smoked.

My mother turned up the music to block out the noise, and we all just sat there waiting for them to come inside. I worried everything was not okay. They were so solid. Why were they fighting? What could be so bad? Probably the houseguests. My mother?

My phone vibrated in my pocket and I pulled it out.

Ava: They are dropping the charges for me and Nick. I'm out of the clinker now! Hope you are OK.

I was so worried she was being charged.

. . .

Me: So relieved! Thank Nick for saving my life. Come visit me soon. I don't think I'll be going to the Cities for a while. Haha!

Ava: You live on the lake, right? I'll be there in the summer. Have somewhere for me to stay, B?

Me: Yes, the perfect place. Chat soon! Love you!

Ava: XO

At least I had some good news today. Ava and Nick were going to be okay. They weren't sitting in jail anymore. I was so relieved.

Victoria and Troy came in about fifteen minutes later with red, swollen eyes. Troy was guiding Aunt Victoria inside by the arm in a sweet and loving way. I never would have believed they were fighting if not for seeing them through the glass and hearing their muffled voices.

They went into their bedroom, and I had a feeling they would not be coming out anytime soon. I needed to get out of the house, despite the cold and darkness outside. I had my camera flashlight, and I would not go far.

I walked down Turtle Creek Road and stopped in front of Tim's driveway. His lights were on. Headlights drew up behind me and moved to the side of the road. The car slowed to a stop.

"What are you doing out here so late?" Tim said.

"Just going for a walk."

"It's cold and snowing," he said.

"I can see that." I stuck my hand out to catch the falling snow, then regretted the snarky words. Even though I could only see him from the shoulders up, he had my heart pounding. He was just so damn handsome. The jerks always were.

"Why don't you walk up my driveway so we can chat for a minute?"

I nodded, and he parked his car in his garage, but left the garage door open.

"So, did you really want a walk in the freezing icy darkness of winter, or did you just need a reason to get out of the house?"

"You got me. It's really cold out here. I needed to get away from family for a little while."

"The holidays can be hard. Want to come inside?"

I stared at him, my body overheating. I followed him inside, but my body was shaking. The damp chill went deep into my bones.

"You're freezing. Come over here by the fire and warm up."

I tried to unzip my jacket, but my fingers were too stiff.

He watched me struggle and took a step to close the gap between us. "Here, let me help."

He unzipped my jacket for me.

How could such a small gesture like unzipping my jacket make my body tremble? Just the slightest feeling of his hands on me, and I was falling for him like a damn fool. He was so good looking that every time I saw him, I blushed. How embarrassing. Why did I swoon over him so much? I was still angry with him for what he did. He was no different from any other guy. I had to shake it off.

Tim patted the spot next to him on the love seat in front of the fire. I thought about sitting somewhere else to prove a point, but who was I kidding? Not when he was inviting me to be in close contact with him.

"Look how fast the snow is falling now," he said, pointing out the window.

"It's sure coming down hard. Looks like we'll get the foot of snow they predicted," I said.

"Or more."

He took my hands in his and held them in front of us so they were closer to the fire.

"I'm so glad you came here tonight. I've been wanting to talk to you about Beth."

I jerked my hands from his grip.

"No. No. It's over between us. Really over. I just need to explain it to you."

"I don't need an explanation. What does she have to do with me?"

He scooted closer to me so our knees were touching.

"I know you're mad, but just hear me out. Beth broke my heart, and I needed some time to process that. When she came crawling back after the guy she cheated on me with cheated on her, I had to make sure it was completely over. I liked you and I didn't want to screw that up."

"You had an awful way of showing it," I said, my nostrils flaring.

"But it wouldn't be fair to you if my mind wasn't completely consumed by you. I really like you, Lizzy. It's over between Beth and me. I want you to know that."

I crossed my arms and pouted like a child. I did not know what to say to him. How could I believe a word he said after the way he acted?

"I came to pick you up and take you to my favorite bakery the next day, but you were gone."

"I went to visit my grandparents in the Cities." Not the complete story, but it was all he needed to know.

"I still plan on taking you there, if you'll go with me."

I was glad he was not smooth with his words. He was all over the place and it made him more human and real.

"What I'm trying to say is, I would love to see where things go with us without any baggage, if you give me another chance."

I held my tongue and sat there in awkward silence. I did not want to give in, but I really did.

"Listen, take your time. This doesn't need to be decided na-now—"

A little stutter slipped out. I leaned toward him, and before I realized what I was doing, my lips were on his. Then my body was on top of his. We rolled to the floor, and I no longer listened to my brain. When we finally pulled apart, we were both gasping for air.

"We should probably slow this down," he said.

I wiped my lips. "You're right. I'm sorry."

"No need to apologize. I wanted it, too."

"I should get going." I put my jacket on and fled to the door. Funny how quick I warmed up in his presence.

"I was planning on coming to Thanksgiving dinner tomorrow if it's okay with you. Your aunt and uncle invited me. But I'll only go if you're okay with it."

He stared at me, no doubt trying to read my expression.

"I guess I'll see you tomorrow, then." I gave him a peck on the lips. My body shivered as I walked out the door without looking back.

Eat your heart out, Tim. I was taking control and walking away. I swayed a little extra with each step. He was watching me out the window. I could feel it, but no way was I going to turn around. It was his turn to suffer.

Chapter Twenty-Six

Victoria

"OH NO, it's Thanksgiving! I can't believe I slept in so late." I jumped out of bed and scanned the floor for my bra and sweatshirt.

"Looking for something?" He said, using my bra as a lasso.

"Stop that. Give me my bra." I reached over, and he pulled me onto the bed and on top of him. The comforter separated his bare skin from mine, but my bra was still held just out of my reach. "Please, Troy. Give it back."

He smiled, a huge teasing smile, as if I hadn't just confessed to him I was dying of cancer. "You need to give me a kiss first."

"Give it back right now, or—"

"Or what?"

I put my finger in his face. "Troy Finney, you give me my bra back right now."

He tickled me. "Only if you give me another kiss."

I rolled my eyes and then gave him a quick peck on the lips as I snatched my bra.

I turned my back to him and dressed.

He watched me intently from the bed.

"Stop staring at me. You know it makes me self-conscious now that I'm all bones."

"You're gorgeous," he said.

He climbed out of the bed and made his way to me. I stopped trying to get dressed as he kissed my shoulder, then worked his way up my neck until I turned around and kissed him on the lips. I wrapped my arms around his head.

If only this moment could go on forever.

"Now, stop setting me up with other women, okay? There's only one girl for me."

He kissed me again. I looked down and smiled.

I would do anything for this man. I loved him so much. When I kissed him, I felt it deep in my soul, and my heart fluttered.

Cooking kept my mind occupied. My mother was by my side, even though she struggled to walk. My sister helped drink the wine, and that was about it. I was glad to have her out of my hair, but I worried about how she would react when I told everyone about my cancer and prognosis.

Lizzy thought I would announce that I was cancer free, but instead I would tell them the exact opposite. I planned to pull her aside before I told everyone, but I never got the chance.

Kat, Maddy, Lyndsey, and Whitney showed up with their families and the turkey.

We had to put two tables together to fit everyone.

"Let's say a prayer, and then we'll go around the table and say what we are thankful for," Troy said.

He never prayed, and it was a surprise when he had everyone say the Lord's prayer as his prayer. I thought it was cute. He knew faith was important to me, and he was trying to make it a part of his life, too.

"I'm thankful for my beautiful wife and everyone here today," Troy said.

"I'm thankful for pumpkin pie," David said.

"I'm so thankful my family is back together for another holiday," my mother said.

"I'm grateful there is more wine," my sister said as she grabbed her glass.

Everyone had their turn until it got to me. I was the last person at the table to speak.

I stood up.

"Some of you may not know I had breast cancer."

No one looked surprised.

"Well, just recently I had some scans completed at the Mayo and my results weren't so good."

All their heads shot up. This, they did not already know.

I cleared my throat. Telling them was so hard.

Troy stood up and took my hand.

"Go ahead, babe."

I nodded and looked around the table at all the people I loved. I owed them the truth. "The cancer has spread to my lymph nodes and my bones. What I'm trying to say is I'm terminal."

David pulled on Maddy's sleeve. "What's terminal, Momma?"

Maddy burst into tears and ran to the bathroom.

I looked down. Everyone was whispering and looked to be in shock.

Lizzy stared at me with so much anger in her eyes. "Why did you lie to me? Why didn't you tell me the truth?"

I should have tried harder to tell her before this. I knew I should have.

"She was scared and wanted some time where no one knew she was sick again and dying," Lyndsey said.

The word dying was a trigger for the table. Lyndsey sat back down, knowing that probably was not the best word to use. She'd drank too much wine to prepare for what was coming.

I took a step toward the bathroom to go after Maddy, but Brad stopped me and said, "I've got this, Victoria. She'll be okay. She will want to be here for you, but right now it just brings back a lot of feelings of sadness."

I wiped the tears from my eyes and nodded. "I know. I'm sorry."

"There is nothing to be sorry for. You did nothing wrong. She just needs a minute." He looked around. "You have enough to deal with right now. I know my wife and she'll be okay." He squeezed my shoulder and slipped past me.

Kat got up and hugged me, along with her daughter, Emma, and the rest of the crew. Maddy came out of the bathroom and ran to me, hugging me tight.

"I'm sorry. It's just—"

"A lot," I said with a small smile.

"A lot," she said as she sat back down. "You mean so much to me. My heart hurts for you."

I knew this would be hard on her. She lost her daughter not too long ago. Now she had to watch one of her best friends pass away slowly.

We all sat and ate small bites.

Maddy moved her food around her plate but never actually raised her fork to her mouth.

Kat broke the silence. "When do you start chemo again?"

I bit my lip, nervous to answer. "I'm not.'

Forks dropped on plates. Half the room gasped, and I felt tears filling my eyes.

Before I could find the words, Troy put his hand on mine to calm me and let me know he had this. He cleared his throat. "There is no cure for Victoria's cancer. We have discussed all her options and we both think that chemo would only land her in a hospital for the time she has left." He paused and wiped his eyes, and his cheeks twitched as he fought to hold a reassuring smile.

I could not look at him. I stared at the table in front of me instead.

"She was in so much pain when she had chemo and since there is very little chance it would work again, she wants to spend this time with all of us instead of being sick and miserable."

The room remained silent.

"I can't believe you will not fight," Diane finally said.

"Mom, the doctors said it will not cure her," Lizzy said.

"It's hard because we all want some hope. We love you so much, dear," my mother said.

I smiled at her. "I love you all so much, and if there was something I could do to get better, I would do it. I'm not giving up. I'm just not going to let chemotherapy kill me."

The room nodded.

Diane grunted. "These are the best doctors in the world and they're telling you to just give up?"

"She's not giving up. She's living her life surrounded by her family," Troy said.

"It's okay, honey," I said. I looked at my friends and family around me at the table. "I know you all care, and I get this may seem like I'm giving up or I've lost hope, but it is the exact opposite. I want to live my last days enjoying everything I have and spend it with all of you. Please don't spend too much time being angry with me. I'd rather spend this time happy with all of you."

Finally, they understood. I could see it in their expressions. The tension dropped in their shoulders, and they all had tears in their eyes.

"What can we do to help?" Emma asked.

"Actually, I have an idea I've been working on for quite some time. It would mean a lot to me if you guys were a part of it."

Everyone looked up at me with hope in their eyes.

My sister just sat there with her arms crossed. She was still angry with me, as to be expected.

"Do you guys want to hear?" I mumbled. They nodded and forced smiles. They had no choice.

"Whatever you need," my dad said.

"First off, I'd like everyone to be here for Christmas, if you can. Second, I made a calendar with the countdown to Christmas. You all know how much I love Christmas."

I winked at Lizzy because she felt the same way, but she was not looking me in the eye or even in my direction. She sat there pushing her food around her plate, but she was not eating.

Tim was sitting next to her. He touched her shoulder, and she finally looked up.

"I've put notes on the calendar boxes of things I want to do to make this the best countdown to Christmas ever. I want you guys to help me open the doors and read the instructions with me and help me finish my bucket list for Christmas. I want to live the rest of my days to the fullest and spend them with you guys."

"This is a lot for everyone to process. I think we need some time," my mother said.

I nodded and cried a little at the thought. "You guys take your time and please eat some dinner. I need to go for a little walk."

Seeing everyone grieving was torture. I needed a break.

No one tried to stop me, but Lizzy followed me. I grabbed my jacket and walked out the door. She did the same.

Once she shut the door, she put her arm around me. "I'm not going to lie, it really hurt when you made the announcement today. You lied to me."

"I know," I said. "And I'm really sorry, but please understand, I needed some time to process it. I just told Troy last night."

Her eyes opened wide. "That was what the two of you were fighting about on the porch?"

I wiped another tear and all I could do was nod. "Everyone heard us, huh? He was not happy with me, that's for sure."

"I'm sorry you're going through this. I'm sorry you felt like you couldn't tell us."

I turned to her. "It's not like that, Lizzy. It's hard to explain. I needed some time to let it sink in first."

She leaned over the railing. "Well, whatever you need, I'm here. You've been here for me with open arms every time I've asked. I'm sad and hurting and numb because I don't want to lose you."

"Oh, sweetheart," I said. "You'll never lose me. I'll always be right here in your heart." I pointed at her chest, and she nodded with understanding.

"It's not fair, Aunt Victoria. It's just not fair. I finally got to know you again. I should have reached out long ago."

"I should have tried harder, too, and I'm sorry. One thing I've learned from all of this is that time is too short and there is nothing more important than family. Please forgive me and help me finish my bucket list. "

She nodded with tears in her eyes.

"And, Lizzy? Promise you will live every day to the fullest because life is just too short."

"I promise," she said. "I'm right here, Aunt Victoria. I'm not going anywhere."

Chapter Twenty-Seven

Lizzy

THE NIGHT finally calmed down a bit after some tears and lots of hugs. We were all in shock and heartbroken. At some point, Troy lost his temper when my mother started making it all about her. He literally kicked her out until he realized there was a snowstorm and she would not make it very far. Kat told mom she could stay at her house, but even Kat did not want her there. She just wanted to get her out of my aunt's hair.

The house had a dark shadow over it now, and the sad news was heavy on our hearts. The thought of Aunt Victoria not being around much longer was on all our minds. It was a lot to take in. She was so positive and trying so hard to make everyone feel better. That was who she was and why it hurt so much.

The snow continued to fall, and I think everyone was grateful they lived just a door or two down, so they could get out of this house, with the exception of grandma and grandpa. Something told me they already knew her secret.

I lay in my bed and stared up at the ceiling. My body was numb. I heard a light knocking on my door and Tim came in.

"How are you doing?"

"As well as can be expected, I guess. I hate that Aunt Victoria has to go through this."

He nodded and sat next to me on the bed. "I don't know your aunt very well, but I have a deep respect for her."

I agreed. "I worry about Uncle Troy. Can you imagine what he's going through? Knowing he'll lose his wife and there is nothing he can do to protect her. It hurts to even think about."

Without saying a word, he climbed on my bed and guided me to lie on his chest. I went with it. He rubbed my head, and we lay there in silence until we both fell asleep. I don't remember the last time I slept that well.

When I woke, Tim was already gone. Good, I did not need all the questions if anyone saw him. They would never believe our night was innocent, comforting.

The snow finally stopped in the morning and my mother, grandma, and grandpa left before dinnertime. My grandparents wanted to get my mother out of here before she started drinking again. I loved my mother, but when she mixed her mental health with alcohol, it never ended well, and I was glad she left. My grandparents were hesitant to leave because they wanted to be with Victoria after such and announcement, but she reassured them that she needed some time.

We ate leftovers that night and played Kings in the Corner until Tim showed up. Immediately, he was forced to play Smear, one of my favorite card games that I'd played with my family as I grew up.

"So, Tim, tell us about yourself. Where are you from?" Victoria asked as she poked her head above the cards to see him.

He cleared his throat and looked at me as I put down the queen of spades, which was the next high in trump suit.

"Nice," he said, watching me closely. We were partners against Troy and Victoria at Troy's insistence.

"I grew up in Duluth and my parents are still together and live in the same home overlooking Lake Superior. I have five sisters, and there isn't too much of a story there. We're just a normal family."

I grabbed my winnings off the table and turned to him. "You think having five sisters is normal in today's world? Did they terrorize you?"

He grinned. "Having that many sisters was not easy, I can tell you that. But I think it helped that I'm the oldest."

His life had me curious about what it was like with that many women in one house. Did they fight over the bathroom? Did it soften him, somehow?

I tapped my fingers on the table, trying to decide my next play. "Do they all live in Duluth, then?"

He put the two of spades on the table and I smiled and grabbed them. "Low," I said.

"Dang it, that's already five points," Troy said. "You guys are killing us."

"No, but they do all live in Minnesota," Tim said, answering my question.

This round I had the Jack and took Victoria's Jick, which was the Jack of clubs.

"That's Jick and Jack, and probably all seven points if we have game," I said.

And after counting our cards, we did.

Tim gave me knuckles.

"They're totally cheating," Troy said. "One more point and you guys win. We might as well call the game now."

"Oh, no you don't," Victoria said. "Us Finneys don't quit."

Uncomfortable silence followed.

Were the rest of them thinking about her giving up on cancer, too? Probably. Her decision bothered me, even it was her choice.

The next hand we played in silence until Tim played low and Troy threw his cards on the table and his head in his hands.

"Good game," Victoria said. "You guys play well together. You may have to teach Troy and me a few things." She looked over at Troy. "Want me to get you a tissue?"

He stuck out his tongue. "That was brutal. How about we watch the Avengers and eat some popcorn?"

Victoria stood up.

We all agreed and followed her into the living room.

As soon as the movie was over, Victoria and Troy announced they were going to bed and Tim said he was going to take off, too.

I walked him to the door and handed him his jacket. "I'm glad you stopped by. I had a lot of fun tonight."

"Me too," he said. "I actually stopped by to invite you to the bakery in the morning. I thought it was long overdue."

I giggled like a high school girl. "Yes, it is. I'd love to."

"Okay. I'll pick you up in the morning, then."

I nodded. "Okay."

I watched him walk down the sidewalk and slowly shut the door when he was finally out of view. Why did he get me so giddy? This was a friendship. A friendship where we liked to snuggle. I really wanted to snuggle with him again. Who was I kidding? I was falling for him.

He arrived at eight on Saturday morning, and a line at the counter had already formed by the time we got to the Black Bear Bakery in Chisholm. The little bakery's creative displays and large variety of pastry were a delight.

"What do you order?"

He looked at me and smiled. "I always get a cinnamon roll and a vanilla latte. How about you? What looks good?"

"I'll get the same."

With so much to choose from, I was struggling to decide. The eclairs and donuts were displayed in an array of colors, and the long johns were perfection. All the bakery looked so delicious. Tim ordered for us, paid, and we sat down at the table to wait.

The bakery was simple but classy and yet comfortable and inviting. The logo caught my eye and was perfect for the area, a black bear riding on a bicycle.

"It's been quite the week for you, hasn't it?" he said, distracting me from my thoughts.

"Quite eventful. Although, it usually is when my mother's around."

Two cinnamon rolls on plates appeared in front of us.

The waitress smiled at us. "Let me know if you need anything else. Enjoy. We are so glad you came by."

I raised my eyebrows at Tim when she walked away. "I'm very impressed by the service here."

"Welcome to Chisholm," he said. "It's just a really tight knit town."

"I can see that." I took a bite, closed my eyes, and moaned. When I opened them, Tim was staring at me, his lips curled into a slow, teasing smile, the corners just barely lifting.

My heart skipped a beat. "What?"

A smile lingered on his lips, and I blushed. "The cute noise you made. It sounded a bit teasing and surprised me, that's all."

I shook my head, but smiled back.

"What are your plans for the rest of the day?"

"Online job hunting, helping Victoria with her advent calendar, and laundry."

He took a bite of his cinnamon roll. "Sounds exciting. If you need any help, company, or support, let me know."

"Sounds good," I said as I took another big bite of the best cinnamon roll I'd ever tasted in my life.

He watched me with an amused expression, food on the end of his fork.

"Stop staring at me. The show is over."

I threw my napkin at him, and he caught it and laughed.

"I have to prepare for the school week today, but then I told Troy I'd come over and help with the Christmas lights," he said.

I nodded my approval. "That is very kind of you. They could use the extra help right now." And I wasn't kidding.

He hardly knew them and was already someone they could count on to help. The friendship in Side Lake was something I had never seen before. The locals all took care of one another. Northern Minnesota was a lot different from southern Minnesota, and it was so refreshing.

We returned to Victoria and Troy's house and the boys spent the day putting up lights. Victoria and I finished painting the wooden calendar. She was in charge of what was in each drawer for the countdown. She kept saying it was a secret, and I was okay with that. I was happy as long as she had a smile on her face.

We ate rice and enchiladas for dinner and we all sat around the kitchen table with red wine and great conversation. I tried not to think about my time with Victoria being limited, but keeping the thoughts out of my mind was difficult. She had become my best friend.

Chapter Twenty-Eight

Victoria

I WOKE UP NAKED AGAIN. This was becoming a habit now. Troy and I had not been this intimate since we first started dating. He could not keep his hands off me, and I felt the same. I had my sex drive back, and I'd never been more attracted to my husband. We did get a bit loud last night. Hopefully Lizzy was a sound sleeper.

I rolled over and kissed his back to wake him. He slowly turned over, opened those beautiful eyes, and reached up to touch my face and pull me in for a kiss.

"Good morning, my beautiful wife."

His lips were a bit swollen, and I laughed at the replay of our night in my mind. Funny how good I slept after a late night with him. Goodbye insomnia.

"You need to get your butt out of bed because it's December first, and you know what that means.".

He kissed me again and then jumped to his feet. "How could I forget?"

I stared at his naked back, and my heart ached for a moment. How many more times would I be able to look at him like this?

I skipped through the hallway and down to the calendar. My body ached, but I did not care because I was on top of the world.

Tim and Lizzy were in the kitchen. Last night, Tim passed out on the couch, and we agreed to let him sleep. He worked so hard helping us decorate the house, he needed to be left to sleep. He was such a good guy and seemed to be getting his priorities sorted out. I had a feeling he and Lizzy would be great together if this relationship between them continued to grow. I was so glad she had someone to be there for her through everything our future held.

I took out my phone to check my texts. Right on time. I sent out a text and then put the calendar in front of Troy. I could barely contain myself. "You get to open the first day."

Every part of me was alive with the anticipation of what was to come.

He pointed at himself and then opened the door carefully.

I covered my mouth with my hands and stood up as I watched him take out the piece of paper, then eye me curiously before reading it silently.

He looked around, frowned, then gazed at me with confusion written all over his face. "I don't get it."

Tim peeked over Troy's shoulder. "What does it say?"

Troy stood up before Tim could get a good look. A knock on the door, and his eyes widened. He had figured it out.

"It says, ruff ruff," Troy said.

I laughed and watched as he opened up the door and turned back around with a dog in his arms and tears in his eyes. Lyndsey came in behind him with a dog carrier and a wagon of dog food.

"Surprise!" Lyndsey said.

"Surprise!" I said, my arms outstretched.

Lizzy clapped her hands. "You guys got a dog?"

"A yellow lab," Tim said, a spring in his step as we all closed in on Troy and the dog.

I rubbed the cute pup under the ears, so tiny in Troy's enormous arms. When I looked back at Troy's face, my eyes instantly clouded.

He had tears running down his face. His expression was mixed with excitement and fear. He knew the reason I got him the dog he always wanted his whole life. I got the puppy to be his new companion when I was gone. To keep him from getting depressed and to warm my side of the bed when I was no longer there.

He put the puppy down, and it ran around the house as if something was chasing it. His feet dragged when he ran too fast for his hind legs to keep up.

Troy grabbed my hand and pulled me to him. He kissed me soft and slow, our lips trembling. His tear slid in between our lips. He pulled away and squeezed me tight.

"Thank you, baby."

I wiped his tears away. "What are we going to name her?"

He bent and picked up the squirming pup and looked up at me. "What about Hope?"

I repeated it in my head. "Hope. I like that. She can be your hunting dog."

He smiled. "Our first fur baby."

Hope fit in with our family from that first day.

Hope had a lot of energy, and the first night she ate a shoe, pooped in my slipper, and woke us up at four in the morning, but she was fun and curious and made Troy smile more than I'd seen him smile in so long. This was the best advent calendar ever.

Not all my friends could be with us when we opened a door each morning, so Lizzy connected all of us by social media. She helped me create a page for live videos so everyone could watch at seven am when we opened another door to the countdown to Christmas.

The next morning was a bit of a surprise when I opened up door two because I totally forgot what I had planned next. I opened it and read it aloud while Lizzy recorded it for our crew. I looked right at the camera with a smile. "Climb the Side Lake fire tower with your friends. You know what this means, guys! We are meeting at four o'clock at the fire tower and you're all coming with me."

Troy's eyes narrowed slightly, and he scanned my face. "But babe, you're afraid of heights."

"Me, too, I'm not doing it," Whitney said from the screen.

"I hate heights," Kat said. "And it's freezing outside."

"Me too, you guys, but we only live once," I said. "Let's do it together. It's not that high. For me, please?"

Yep, I was using the dying girl look to make them come with me, but this was the whole point. To come together as friends and bond. To experience new things together. Even when the experiences were a bit out of our comfort zone.

When the silence continued for longer than comfortable, I said, "I wanted to challenge myself and you guys, too. We can do this together."

"Fine. If you do it, I'll do it," Kat said.

"Me too," Whitney said. "Whatever you need. We're here for you."

Everyone agreed. It warmed my heart that my friends were willing to face their fears for me, but then again, they had little choice in the matter.

We met at the fire tower. Kevin had arranged for the chain and padlock to be removed.

"The Side Lake lookout was used to triangulate the location of fires in the past. Now it's a landmark and a spectacular view," Troy said. "Although, I believe it's still used when wildfire danger is high."

The fire tower had a flight of stairs, a platform, another flight of stairs, and another platform. That pattern continued to repeat quite a few times, but I never counted how many flights from the bottom.

"I believe it's about fifteen stories high," Kevin said, as if reading my mind. "Right around one hundred and fifty feet."

We walked up the stairs, one at a time, but the guys soon raced ahead. Us women stayed behind and plodded up to the tower together. Today was one of my better days, but I was still weak, so we took a lot of breaks before we made it to the top.

"My grandma told me my grandpa used to climb the outside of this tower with his brothers, and they would hang from it. Absolutely no fear of heights," Kat said.

Lyndsey snorted. "And no common sense."

Kat laughed. "Very true. I can't believe none of them died. They would play tag. No rules."

"Wow, and I'm dizzy just climbing the stairs," I said. "I couldn't imagine climbing on the outside."

"That's so dangerous," Maddy said.

Kat and Maddy were the only two women who weren't out of breath by the time we reached the top.

I had to bend over to catch my breath before facing the edge. Kat and Whitney grabbed my hands, and I squeezed them both as we nervously walked to the viewing wall-sized window. I took a deep breath and held onto the railing to feel stable.

The view actually took my breath away. A smile spread across my face.

I felt something deep inside as I stared at the trees, now white with snow and the frozen lake in the distance. The surreal vision took my breath away.

Whitney pointed. "Big Sturgeon."

"And there," Kat said as she pointed. "That narrow strip of land is the campground."

"I can see my house from here," Whitney said. She was the only one of us who did not live on Turtle Creek Road.

"I can only imagine what it will look like in the summer with green trees and blue water," Lizzy said.

I closed my eyes and let the freezing wind blow my hair back. This was my moment.

I let go of the railing and held onto Kat and Whitney's hands, and Whitney grabbed onto Lizzy, and Lizzy took Maddy's hand and Maddy clasped Kat's hand. The guys closed in on us and put their arms around our shoulders from behind.

I would never forget this beautiful moment. "Time for photos."

I took out my phone and snapped some pictures of us. I wanted everything about this day to last long after I was gone. I needed to do something special so they would never forget who I was.

Chapter Twenty-Nine

Lizzy

I HAD no idea how much the advent calendar would affect me. The calendar became something exciting to wake up to every morning. I'd applied for jobs, but I'd also applied for the nursing program at the Minnesota North Hibbing campus. If I got in for the fall, I'd apply for grants and scholarships. When I found a job, I would save up, so I did not end up with so much student loan debt by the time I earned my degree. My life was turning around.

If Minnesota North accepted me, I could become a nurse and work in a hospital. Nursing school would be a challenge, but I could do it with hard work and dedication. My dream was working with children in pediatrics. I had forgotten what it was like to dream again, but watching someone like Victoria live her dreams with limited time made me realize anything was possible. I was grateful for the life I had.

I was ready to start believing in myself after watching Aunt Victoria and how she dealt with her prognosis with such grace and optimism. She was my role model. Her bravery inspired me. She woke up every morning with a smile on her face, even though I could tell the pain was getting worse.

I lived with her, so I knew she was exhausted and weak. She played it off and pushed herself, but she was focused on living each day to the fullest, in case it was her last day. Sometimes she forgot to stop and rest. I worried this would catch up with her later on and at some point she would just drop, but she was smart and she was making this choice. I needed to support her.

At the end of the first week of the advent calendar, we had built a snowman, gone snowmobiling, sledding at the Side Lake rec center, taken photos for a Christmas card Victoria set up, and yesterday we had a snowball fight.

I loved counting down to Christmas, but for the first time, I did not want Christmas to come because the calendar would end.

The Side Lake crew treated me like family. They were my family. But a part of me worried that when Victoria was gone, I would no longer have a place here anymore. I would not stay in this house with Troy without her, and I had no other place to live. Side Lake did not have low income apartments. I'd be moving to Hibbing and finding a place closer to school when the time came. Would I lose my new family?

So, I soaked up every minute with them and enjoyed each exciting morning where Victoria opened up the calendar, as if for the first time.

I wanted to do something for Victoria. Something big to show her how much I loved her and how much I appreciated all she'd done for me. I had an idea, but I'd needed a team to make it work.

Whitney read the next note. "Go to Bentleyville in Duluth."

"I've never been there," Victoria said. "I heard so much about it. I thought it would put us all in the Christmas spirit."

"I've never been there either," I said. "I can't wait."

We drove two vehicles to Canal Park in Duluth. By the time we reached the top of the hill in Duluth, darkness had blanketed the city. We drove down the huge hill and through downtown to Canal Park, and that's when we saw the beautiful multi-colored display of lights at Bentleyville.

"It's the largest free walk-through lighting display," Brad said. "All we have to do is pay for parking, although they take donations.."

"I never think it feels like Christmas until I see Bentleyville," Lyndsey said.

"We never missed a Christmas here," Tim said. "Although, it isn't too far from my parents' house. You can see the lights from there."

"That's cool," Ethan said.

"How did this even come about?" I said to no one in particular.

"Well, in 2001, I believe, a man named Nathan Bentley had a love for Christmas and decorated his house in Esko for the holiday," Tim said with deep passion.

Obviously, this place meant a lot to him.

"The next couple of years he added more and more lights until he had so many. He created a lighting display that attracted many people to drive by and admire. His house became known as "the house with all the lights in Esko.""

"I know he attracted more people after a couple of years by changing his display so people could walk through instead of driving by. Santa Claus even made appearances for the children on the weekends," Kevin said.

David clapped his hands. "Santa ho ho!"

Three-year-old David loved repeating what we said, so we had to be careful when we were around him. I'd learned quickly.

"A friend of Nathan's jokingly compared Bentleyville to Whoville from Dr. Seuss's book. People loved the lights, and the display soon became the Bentleyville Tour of Lights. Nathan and his family moved to Cloquet into a bigger home around 2004, and his new home became even more popular. He made a six foot by four-foot castle in his new home for the entrance and had close to forty or fifty thousand lights. Hundreds of snowflakes hung from trees and he added new light displays every year." Kevin smiled as he looked up at the lights.

Bentleyville must have played a big part in his childhood, too. I loved how something like this could bring us all together to enjoy.

"I couldn't have said it better myself. Don't forget the fire pits," Tim said. "Visitors could roast marshmallows and see Santa Claus every night and he would pass out free winter hats and bags of cookies."

"I love that," I said. "You guys sound a bit like a brochure. Maybe you guys should give tours."

They beamed with pride.

Brad took the lead as we walked through the parking lot. "They still do that, but the way."

"Do what?" I asked.

"Give out cookies and hot cocoa and stuff for free," he said.

"Remember, he had that cookie house and gave out free cookies and apple cider? He even had paved walking paths," Troy said as he reached down to pick up David.

Tim put his arm around me, and I didn't fight it. "My favorite part was the popcorn building," Tim said. "They gave out free popcorn to everyone as they walked by."

I looked at him. "Why did they move the displays to Canal Park?"

"Because it was so popular there was no parking and horrible traffic congestion on the street," he said. "Thirty-five thousand people had visited his new house in just two years. They tried bussing people in, and it stayed there another five years, but in 2008 Nathan closed it down to figure out a new way to make it work."

"The next year, the mayor of Duluth called Nathan and suggested the display move to Bayfront Festival Park, right?" Lyndsey asked. "They had more than enough room and parking. It kept Nathan's dream alive but with the help of the city."

Both Kevin and Tim nodded.

Kevin pointed at Mr. and Mrs. Claus and the kids got in line with their parents as we stood and chatted. "It opened here in 2009, right after Thanksgiving and was four times bigger than before and had millions of lights. Every year it keeps getting bigger. Mr. and Mr. Claus now skydive in on opening night and fireworks end the final night every season."

"Wow, that's amazing," I said. "We have nothing close to this in the Cities."

"If I had known about the skydiving Santa and Mrs. Claus, I would have suggested we come on opening night," Victoria said with a crack in her voice.

I could hear the worry in her voice, as if she was thinking she probably wouldn't be alive next year to see the skydiving Santa. We all thought it but no one said it, and no one wanted to think it could really be true.

The display was right next to Lake Superior, and the lights reflected off the lake. We looked up at the mesmerizing Christmas tree lights.

Victoria was in tears and we joined in a group hug, appreciating this moment with her.

Hot cocoa was next on the tour. Victoria raised her cup. "Here is to the best friends a girl could ever ask for. This is a day I will never forget."

"Cheers," we all said and raised our glasses.

David and Brittany were full of giggles and sang Christmas songs as we walked through the gigantic light display.

Who knew life could be so much more than what I'd settled for? This was where I was supposed to be.

Chapter Thirty

Victoria

I HAD such a wonderful night at Bentleyville with my favorite people on this earth. The only problem was it really exhausted me. Twice Troy asked me how I was doing and both times I put a smile on my face, but he saw right through it.

I loved hearing the stories about Bentleyville from the guys. The light display was a big part of their upbringing and childhood memories, which made it even more special.

I passed out the minute I got into the car, and Troy had to carry me into the house. I was so exhausted I could not put one foot in front of the other.

The next morning, I struggled to get out of bed, but the excitement of the calendar made me push through the pain. I had Lizzy open the calendar because it was one she'd love.

"Girls night!" she said.

We slept over at my house and Troy slept at Kevin's house. We had an amazing night of drinking, board games, and watching the *High*

School Musical movies in order. I was sprawled on the pullout in my living room with Lyndsey. Maddy, Emma, and Kat were laying on the l-shaped couch, and Lizzy and Whitney were plopped on the recliners.

I was putting the second *High School Musical* movie on my old school DVD player when Maddy asked how I was feeling.

"I love how positive and happy you are. You're an inspiration to all of us." Maddy looked around the room and everyone agreed.

"But we're worried about you. How are you feeling?" Kat asked.

This was exactly what I wanted to avoid.

"Be honest," Lyndsey said.

That was so hard for me to do. I sighed. "You really want to know?"

They all nodded.

"Please," Lizzy said. "I think we want to make sure you're okay."

"Okay. The truth is, I'm having more fun than I've ever had in my life. I'm living each day like it is my last, and I feel like I've gotten closer to all of you. I hate that I don't know how long I have, but I appreciate every day on this earth so much more. I'm not worried all the time about small things like bills and how I look. I don't take so much time to get ready and put on makeup and go shopping." I paused to smile at them. "Every minute is so important, and I think hard about how I really want to spend each day."

"I don't worry so much about what everyone else is thinking about me anymore, either," Lyndsey said. "You've made me look at life in a different way."

"You should never care about the judgement others have about you. It would hurt way too much, and does it matter at the end of the day?" I asked the girls.

My dear friends shook their heads.

"I love my sister and I really want to make things right between us." I looked at Lizzy and she smiled at my confession. "I want her to be okay when I'm gone. I want to help her give up drinking for good and live her life. That's really what I want."

"I agree one hundred percent, but it's no use," Lizzy said. "I've tried for years."

I got up and kneeled next to her recliner. "This is my Christmas wish. I want all of us together without any fighting."

She nodded, staring off as I turned toward my friends.

"But how are you feeling?" Maddy asked.

"I'm exhausted and weak, and I struggle to feel beautiful at times with this unwanted disease wiping out my existence, and I hate that I can't do anything about it. I hate that I'm going to leave Troy all alone."

My puppy whined and pouted as if she knew what was happening to me. She walked over to me and sat down with her chin on my leg. I petted her sweet little head.

"I want to have fun and spend every day with you. With Troy. That's what makes me happy and brings me joy. And I can't wait until Christmas. I want to have a big party with all of you."

"I won't be here for Christmas but I'd love to spend New Year's with you," Whitney said. "We promised Josh's family we would go there this year."

"I'll be here," Lizzy said. "I'm not super happy about my mother coming, but for you, I'll make sure she does."

My eyes teared up, and I reached out for her hand. "Thank you."

"I promise we'll take care of Troy after you're gone. He won't be alone," Kat reassured me.

"We've got you," Lyndsey said. "Although it's hard sometimes, I want you to know you can talk to me about anything at all."

I stared up at her. "Even if it's my wish after I'm gone?"

She rolled her eyes and crossed her arms. "Not if it is about setting Troy up with another woman. Please don't make me do that ever again."

I laughed. "You're such a whiner."

She threw her pillow at me.

"Don't worry. I'm past that," I said, dodging it. "He found out and was so pissed off. I realized I was trying to be selfless, but I guess I didn't take Troy's opinion into consideration."

"What? You did what?" Maddy said, her voice squealing.

"It's not a big deal. I may have created a dating profile for Troy online and one of his old friends from his childhood may have reached out to him after she saw it."

Lyndsey shook her head. "And she may have been the doctor from the grief support group Victoria dragged me to."

Kat's eyes narrowed. "Grief support group? Who died?"

Lizzy's lips parted as she blinked rapidly, trying to understand. "Wait, like you two went to process your feelings with other people who lost someone?"

This sounded so much worse out loud. They'd never understand. "Not exactly. After I found out I was terminal, I drug Lyndsey to a grief support group to try to find Troy a replacement wife. It didn't work out so well."

Their eyes widened at my words.

"Like you thought you could easily be replaced?" Kat said. "By a grieving widow?"

I gave her credit for being blunt all the time, but not this time. This time, her bluntness was too much and it hurt. "I know it was stupid, but I thought I was being a good wife at the time."

"It's not stupid. It's just surprising because Troy loves you so much. You aren't replaceable, Victoria. He worships the ground you walk on," Kat said.

"It's true," Whitney said. "You two have a great relationship and friendship. He'll never move on from you. Not in that way. He may find someone else to share his life with, but they won't be you. You're the love of his life."

Lyndsey stood up. "It's true. And it's the last thing on his mind. He doesn't need anyone to make him happy. You make him happy. Now, who needs some ice cream?"

Everyone cried out, "Yes!"

Maybe they were right. Maybe I did not need to set him up after I was gone. He'd one day find someone else, but he would always have room in his heart for me, too. I was there first.

Chapter Thirty-One

Lizzy

THE NEXT WEEK WAS MAGICAL. We bought a dozen red poinsettia bouquets with a beautiful arrangement of white roses from Range Floral in Hibbing because Maddy insisted they were the best and always the most creative arrangements and the freshest flowers. We pulled up at random houses in Side Lake to hand them out.

We all crammed into Maddy and Brad's three row SUV and went around knocking at random doors that looked like people lived in year round. There had to be tracks in the snow. We took turns running up, knocking on the door, and handing them a Christmas bouquet.

Their faces lit up, and it felt so gratifying to hand the bouquets out. I got to give out two bouquets, and the first one was a little old lady who struggled to walk, so I took the bouquet into her house and set it on her table. She asked me to stay for a cup of coffee and Christmas cookies, but I told her we had more flowers we needed to deliver. She wanted me to come back some other time, and I promised I would.

Knocking on a random door and giving out beautiful flowers to strangers was so gratifying. The excitement of the person behind the door when they saw the lovely flowers filled my heart. Victoria gave out the last one to Dawson Kirsich and his wife, Emily. He was a teacher at Dylan Elementary. They had sweet kids and such a beautiful home from the outside. I could only imagine what it looked like inside.

I loved exploring Side Lake and seeing all the places I'd never seen. The town was much bigger than I expected, and some of the houses were so creative. Brad pointed out Kevin McHale's house and McCarthy's Beach, which was the most popular public beach around the area.

We went Christmas caroling another night. I nearly froze. That night was not one of my favorite nights. We struggled to sing as a group and lacked practice and collaboration. Some of us were off key, and we were all over the place. But I never laughed so hard.

Brad was being Brad and ran through the snow with David on his back until it got too cold, and they took all the kids to Kat's house where her daughter Emma volunteered to watch them. I had a feeling she was embarrassed to be caroling with us, and I did not blame her. We sounded terrible.

We were walking toward Bimbos because Brad had the great idea of singing there. We were just two blocks away when Tim put his arm around me and squeezed me in, lightly kissing the top of my head.

He was so gentle and kind, and the most beautiful man I'd ever laid eyes on.

He looked over at Victoria to make sure she was out of earshot.

"How's the party planning going?"

"It's really hard to do it without her knowing, but I'm having so much fun. Everyone has been so helpful, and now I don't feel like it's all on me. It's going to be perfect. I haven't asked you yet, but will you play your guitar and sing at the party?"

He smiled and kissed my hand. "Anything for Victoria. She's never going to forget this, you know that? What you're doing for her is incredible."

She would be so happy, but we were running out of time. Her health was declining and the circles around her eyes were getting darker. But we would make sure this Christmas was the best she ever had. I always loved Christmas, but this year I was looking at it in a whole new light. Time to forgive and move on from my past. To open up my heart instead of closing it.

Kevin ran ahead of us to open the door to Bimbo's.

Tim looked at me. "Ready?"

"This will be rough," I said with a laugh.

And it was.

Except everyone sang with us, so it really wasn't so bad. The staff, the customers, all of us sang three Christmas songs before leaving. Once we stopped, the owner made a toast to Victoria, and Troy picked her up like a bride and swung her around.

She was glowing. Someone grabbed a garland off the wall and wrapped it around her neck like a scarf. She smiled from ear to ear when Troy sat her down.

On the way home, he gave her a piggyback ride. That was true love.

On Sunday, we made Christmas cookies in the shape of candy canes and gooey marshmallow wreaths. We frosted sugar cookies shaped like Santa Claus, bells, Christmas trees, and reindeer. We played Dolly and Kenny, and of course, Alabama. We laughed, we cried, and we sang loud and proud. Victoria was on top of the world, and she and Troy seemed closer than ever.

On Monday, we had game night, but halfway through Monopoly, Victoria snuck away to go to bed. The circles under eyes continued to darken, and Troy had to assist her in walking.

On Tuesday, us women had our first book club meeting and on Wednesday, we all rang the bell for the Salvation Army. Victoria was close to an hour late for book club and only showed up for the last fifteen minutes of bell ringing, Troy pushed her into Casey Drug in a wheelchair. She was very apologetic she was late to ring the bell, but we all knew she was struggling just to get out of bed. Her health was declining rapidly.

The end was coming much sooner than I expected, and the realization weighed heavy on my chest. I did not want to believe it, but she was slowing down more each day, and she was in so much pain.

Some days she would have so much energy, like on Thursday when we all drove to Nashwauk for group photos at Appletree Photography.

Lyndsey insisted it was the best place around, and they really were. Our photos were adorable. We all laughed and smiled with Santa hats and sexy gowns. When I came home, my stomach hurt from all the jokes. Everything we did together was so much fun.

We had another day of photos with Santa on Friday at the rec center during the annual winter festival. There were horse-drawn sleigh rides, dogsled rides, kids and adults figure skating, sledding, snowshoeing, inside games for the kids, arts and crafts, and bon-fires with hot cocoa and snacks.

Victoria sat a lot and watched everyone else because she was too weak to volunteer. Troy pushed her around the skating rink in her wheelchair at the end of the party, and she laughed so hard. She continued to make the best of every day.

"This is already the best holiday season I've ever had. Costa Rica and even South Africa couldn't hold a candle to the Christmas season in Side Lake," Victoria said.

I could not imagine a Christmas without snow. The seasons were a pleasant change for all of us.

The next morning we didn't open a door on the advent calendar because Victoria insisted everyone meet in person after dinner to open it instead. No kids were allowed. I was quite curious what this one could be. I snuck away most of the day to Kat's house to help with the cooking and decorating for Victoria's special Christmas surprise party.

I looked at Kat as we untangled more lights for the outdoor Christmas display. "What do you think she could have planned that no kids are allowed?"

Kat laughed. "I don't know, but I know she had Troy buy one of those big outdoor saunas they had professionally installed a few days ago. Right down by the water."

"You think she wants to have a sauna party?"

She shook her head. "It has to be more than that, but yes. She just sent a group text that said we need to bring our suits and towels, so my guess is a sauna is part of it."

"I didn't notice they had it installed, and I live there."

"You've been preoccupied throwing this surprise Christmas party for Victoria, which is brilliant, by the way. I wish I had thought of it first, so I got all the credit. You're going to be her favorite person, you know."

"We all planned this together. But I think you're right. She's going to freak out."

Kat glowed. "This will be the best Christmas she's ever had. It's her dream Christmas. I can't wait to see her face when she gets here."

"Me too."

Chapter Thirty-Two

Victoria

"AS YOU ALL KNOW, this is the last night before Christmas Eve and I wanted it to be special." I held up the advent calendar on the table. "A few days ago, Troy and I got a sauna, as some of you already know."

"We guessed that's why you wanted us to bring our suits."

I winked at them. "Well, you know I always have a twist."

Kevin raised an eyebrow. "There's a twist to the sauna?"

"Yes. I'll tell you more once we're all in there."

I turned away before anyone asked any more questions. I had to tell Troy my plan since I needed his help to do something I could not manage on my own.

Most of us already had our suits on under our clothes as we made our way down to the new sauna.

It could fit up to twelve people comfortably. We probably paid a little too much for it.

"This sauna is huge," Josh said, stepping aside to show his wife

Whitney. He touched the wood, and she did the same. "Is this Red Cedar?"

"Sure is," Troy said. "Victoria picked it out. It's actually Harvested Canadian Clear Western Red Cedar."

"Ooh, sounds expensive," Josh said. "I love it."

We walked inside to the two-tier benches with rounded front corners. The cedar grill was on the outside of the tempered glass windows in the entryway, where everyone stopped to take off their clothes.

I was dripping with sweat after just a minute or two in the sauna. It warmed up fast.

"Okay guys, the surprise is Troy drilled a giant hole in the ice so we can jump into the frozen lake when we get hot."

"I haven't done that since I was a kid," Brad said, excitement in his voice. "Lynz, do you remember when we got mom and dad to jump in that one year with us?"

"I couldn't believe mom did it. It was pretty awesome."

"Your mom? I can see your dad," Kevin said. "But not your mom."

This was the perfect opportunity to be convincing. "If Lyndsey and Brad's mom can do it, so can you guys."

"It's going to be so cold. Do we have to?" Maddy said with a whimper.

"You'll be just fine. Remember when Kevin made us go late night skinny dipping last year? I think we've got this. And it's easier because everyone gets to wear a suit," I said.

"I can't believe I'm doing this," Josh said. "But anything for you."

I smiled.

Everyone started talking, and Troy took it as the perfect opportunity to put his arm around me. "How are you feeling? Do you think you'll be okay doing this?"

"I think so. Just jump in with me and be there to help me out, okay?"

He kissed me. "I'm here for you, babe."

After I turned on the outdoor light, everyone took turns jumping in the lake and running back to the sauna. Troy and I were last. They all came out in towels to watch. Lizzy was shaking.

"That is the craziest thing I've ever done!" she said.

"I can't believe you did a cannon ball," Tim said. "Actually, I can believe it. You're crazy."

She laughed and grabbed his hand.

I smiled at them. They were hitting it off again. I loved to see it. I'd known for a while they'd be the perfect match.

Troy turned to me and threw his towel at Josh. "Ready?"

I squealed with excitement and dropped my towel in the snow.

"I'm ready. 1-2-3!"

Troy picked me up and ran fast to the hole, then stopped and jumped in with me in his arms. I screamed as we hit the water together. Troy did not let go of me.

It took a minute for the shock of the cold water to numb my body. My feet were so cold. Troy handed me to Kevin, and he ran me back to the sauna with a towel covering me. I didn't even protest because I would never get there fast enough on my own. And I did not want to freeze my feet in the cold snow.

The heat of the sauna was a shock to my body, but it took the chill out pretty quick and I could feel my fingers and feet again.

"Do you think we got frostbite?" I said to no one in particular.

"Nah, we weren't out there long enough," Kevin said.

That night, I crashed hard. I fell asleep when my head hit the pillow after a nice hot bath and I did not wake until the sun brightened my room and woke me.

I smiled because it was Christmas Eve morning.

My sister and my parents showed up close to noon. I was worried they would not come because my sister had not talked to me since the day she stormed out of here on Thanksgiving. She still avoided talking to me when she arrived, and she complained about everything from the sheets not being soft enough to the house being too cold.

She grunted when she opened the fridge and looked over at me. "I can't believe you only have white bread in here. Don't you know it's all sugar?"

"Maybe you should go grocery shopping for your kind of bread,

Diane," my mother said. "We wouldn't want Victoria to fill up on sugary bread now, would we? Good thing she has you to keep her healthy."

I struggled to keep a straight face.

I could not remember the last time I kept down a piece of bread. I sometimes dreamed of carbs. I ate nothing other than a soup broth lately and even that was hard to swallow.

"I wish I could get her to eat bread," Troy said. "I'd make her a pie for breakfast if she could keep it down."

My sister looked me up and down. "You look even skinner than you did at Thanksgiving. You know thin isn't in anymore, right?"

I knew she meant it as an insult, but I found it rather funny. She knew why I was boney and it wasn't because I wanted to look good. I had to remind myself the anger inside her from the shock of my cancer made her say such things. Maybe she was scared to admit I was dying, and she wanted to pretend it would not happen.

Everyone disappeared shortly after lunch. They all had different places to go. I was left watching the potica in the oven to make sure it did not burn. My mother said she needed to lie down before dinner and Kat was busy cooking Christmas Eve dinner at her house. She told me I needed to take it easy, but the truth was I loved to cook at Christmas, and I was sad about the whole thing. Dad sat in his wheelchair, asking one-hundred questions about our remote control because they still had not tried streaming. They loved cable and wanted no part in Wi-Fi or smart televisions.

The day dragged on, and I was ready to go to sleep at five when Troy came in and asked if I was ready to go. I'd put on my sparkly Christmas dress with a black cardigan and I had even put on makeup and curled my hair for the first time in a long time. We were going to church with our friends for my favorite holiday of the year. Kat and Lizzy said they were too busy with dinner to come, and it broke my heart. Whitney and Josh were not around, and Kevin could not get it off work. Didn't they know this was probably my last Christmas?

My favorite part about church on Christmas Eve was the candlelight ceremony as we sang *Silent Night*. It would not be the same without all my friends there.

Something did not seem right. My friends were not like this. Why didn't they care? Maybe I pushed too hard with the advent calendar? Whatever the reason, it hurt.

We left the church, and I dreaded going to Kat's house. I was exhausted, and my heart was broken that not everyone was at church or able to make it for Christmas at all. They were my people, and they were not able to spend one night at church with me?

I was overreacting, of course. They'd been there for me through the advent calendar, facing their fears and being by my side. They were so supportive, and I was so grateful for every one of them, but I also felt broken.

It was Christmas and my people were not with me. I just wanted to skip Christmas Eve. My legs were shaking with exhaustion, and my eyes were heavy. "Can we go home for a while? I'm not really feeling up for the Christmas celebration tonight."

Troy looked over at me with concern in his eyes and it weighed heavy on my heart.

"Christmas is your favorite holiday of the year, sweetheart. Are you sure you don't want to at least say hello to everyone?"

I turned away to hide my tears. He pulled the car over and put his hand on my shoulder. "Baby, look at me."

I couldn't. I wouldn't.

"What's wrong?" he whispered. "You're worrying me. Is it your stomach? Your head?"

I shook my head but still could not look his way.

"What is it, Victoria?"

I tried so hard to swallow the lump in my throat, but I burst out crying into my hands. He jumped out of the car and ran around to open my door. I didn't realize he had stopped the car in Kat's long driveway.

I sobbed into his shoulder. "I just want to go home. My friends didn't t care enough to come to church with me. They've been distant. It doesn't feel like Christmas. I want to go home. I'm so exhausted."

He held me tight.

"Listen, I'm not supposed to tell you this, but before we leave I want you to know not all your friends made it to church tonight because they've been busy throwing you a surprise Christmas party. Whitney and Josh are here for Christmas. They wanted it to be a surprise. They didn't go anywhere. And Kevin isn't really working."

"What?" I could not believe my ears. "They were planning a Christmas party for me?"

"I helped, but it was all Lizzy's idea. She wanted to do something special for you, and she knows how much Christmas means to you. They're all waiting for you to arrive."

I laughed through the tears. "I'm such an idiot. Now I'm going to show up there all puffy eyed with mascara streaming down my face. You should have told me."

He kissed me and held my face in his hands. "I didn't want to ruin their surprise. I love you so much. If you're tired, I can—"

"No! I'm a fool, but I want to go. I can't believe they planned a party for me. Will there be live music? A mistletoe? Santa Claus?"

He kissed me again. "You've already made me ruin the surprise. Just wait and see."

"Fine," I said. "Let's go!"

Chapter Thirty-Three

Lizzy

WE WATCHED them pull up in front of Kat's garage. I sent out a group text and waited behind the tree as Victoria's door opened and all the lights lit up, illuminating a path that took her and Troy into the woods.

I ran around to meet them, making sure everything was in place.

She gasped as she walked through the manger scene, her arm entwined with Troy's. She struggled to walk by herself without some assistance now. Then she saw the elves placed alongside the path. Once she got to the gazebo, she cried out and hugged Troy tight.

It brought tears to my eyes as he led her to the sleigh and helped her in. We had snow lights hanging from the trees, the sleigh decorated with lights, and a big sack of presents on the floor.

We all came walking out of the woods and turned on the battery powered candles we held in our hands. I turned on the light that shone on Tim, sitting in a chair on a red carpet.

I grabbed the microphone and gave it to Troy as he sang Merry

Christmas to You, to Victoria. She cried and wow, I knew he was going to sing, but I had no idea how beautiful his voice was. I knew he and Tim had been practicing together, but he blew me away and left me with goosebumps.

At the very end, he got down on one knee and I ran over to take the microphone and hand him the box.

He nodded and mouthed a thank you in my direction and opened it up in front of Aunt Victoria.

"Victoria Finney, you have changed my whole life for the better. Before I met you, I never appreciated Christmas. It was a time of sadness and stress for me and then you came along and I fell in love with everything about the holiday. You are my Mrs. Claus. Will you do me the honor and marry me again?"

"Yes!"

He opened up the box, and she squealed with excitement. Josh took pictures and Lyndsey placed the Santa coat on Troy and Santa hats on both of them.

Kevin was dressed in a reindeer costume with big antlers as he opened up a Bible. The costume was hideous, really. Then he put on the glowing red nose, and we all broke out in laughter.

Victoria leaned forward and pushed the button on the side of his nose, and it started blinking.

"I'm sorry, but it's very hard to take you seriously with that thing on." She was hunched over, trying to catch her breath. She finally stood up and Troy took her hands in his.

They stared into each other's eyes as Kevin officiated.

After the ceremony, Troy bent her back and kissed her in the most beautiful and elegant way. A mistletoe hung right above their heads. There wasn't a dry eye around as the kiss went on and on.

They finally stood upright again, and we crowded in for hugs.

Victoria put her arm in mine. "I know this was your idea, and I want to thank you, Lizzy."

My mother came out from behind me and hugged Victoria. "I'm sorry I have been so terrible to you. I want you to know I'm done drinking. I've had a hard time understanding why you wouldn't tell us, but

I'm sorry. It wasn't my decision to make, and I've wasted too much time hating you."

They hugged, and for the first time in a long time, I was proud of my mother.

Victoria whispered something to Troy, and he ran out to his car and brought in a sack of presents.

"I got each and every one of you a gift to remember me by. I love you all so much, and I never want you to forget me. You've been there for me during the hardest days of my life, and you're all here today. I can't even explain how much that means to me."

A beautiful woman I'd never met before came walking down the path in front of Victoria. She started laughing and crying at the same time. They hugged, then the woman took the microphone

Victoria held her hand and the microphone. "Everyone, meet Dr. Danny Orlando."

Lyndsey walked up to the doctor and hugged her. "No way. Is this for real? What are you doing here?"

The doctor had an arm around each of them.

"Victoria reached out and invited me here for Christmas. She knew my husband had passed away, and I didn't have any family. I'm so happy to be here tonight."

Lyndsey turned toward Victoria and put a hand on each of her shoulders to steady herself. "Tell me you didn't, Victoria. You promised me."

Troy stepped forward. "It's okay. She's just a friend. Victoria asked me first. Danny was like a sister to me growing up."

Lyndsey's body loosened at his words. "Thank the Lord." She turned around and grabbed a glass of champagne off the picnic table.

Kat placed a pitcher of eggnog on the table.

It was time for a little fun at Tim's expense. I walked over and filled two cups, then took them over to Tim, who sat on a chair next to the microphone with his guitar in his hands.

"Oh, no," he said, pushing the plastic cup away.

"I told you I would make you try it."

"Nope. Not a chance." He covered his nose and his mouth and turned his head.

"Don't be a baby. Try it for me?" I gave him a sad puppy dog look. "If you do this, I will forgive you and give you another shot."

"You'll spend New Years with me and be my girlfriend," he said, flashing that killer smile my way.

"Fine," I said.

He clinked his cup against mine and downed the whole cup. He wiped his mouth and shot me a sly grin. "The truth is I love eggnog, but I wanted to use it to my advantage someday by telling you I didn't."

"You jerk!" I cried out and chased him into the house. "You're going to pay, big time, mister."

After I finally caught him, he kissed me and we went back outside. I looked over his shoulder at Victoria, who smiled my way.

I walked toward her and grabbed her hand.

"That smile looks good on you," she said.

I felt my cheeks blush. "What smile?"

"That smile you have when you are with him. You light up the entire room, you know."

"Is it that obvious?"

She nodded and coughed. "You found your happy ending. Promise me you will believe in yourself and finish school and let him in. Give him your heart, Lizzy."

My eyes filled with tears. "Sometimes I hear that voice in my head telling me I'm not good enough for him, and I'm not smart enough to be a nurse."

"You are good enough, smart enough, and don't you ever stop believing in yourself. Promise me. Promise me you will let yourself be loved and you won't push him away when things get serious."

"I promise." I kneeled next to her wheelchair, my knees in the snow but I didn't care. "You have been like a mother to me and I'll never forget your kindness. If it wasn't for you, I don't know where I'd be. Thank you, Victoria. I knew I could always count on you."

"I always believed in you, Lizzy. Never let anyone make you think any different."

Epilogue

Troy

"TAKE one more sip and tell me what you think," I said, putting the white coffee cup in front of Kevin.

"You're going to give me a heart attack. Do you know how many lattes you have pushed down my throat in the past hour?"

I dug my palms into my eyes. "I just want everything to be perfect."

The door opened, and the bell rang.

Lyndsey peeked her head around the door and walked in once she saw us by the counter. "How's it going? Are you ready for the grand opening? Is there anything you need me to do?"

I shook my head. It didn't feel right to open the coffee shop without Victoria. She was taken too soon. I struggled to get out of bed this morning. I glanced over at the new and used books that lined the shelves. Kat, Lyndsey, and Maddy helped to organize the books. I had not planned on having the bookstore, but it was my way of keeping Victoria's dream alive.

Today marked four months since she passed away. That day will forever be embedded in my mind. It was the day my wife left this world, but also the day she stopped hurting. Today was the tenth of May. Spring. The snow was finally gone, and a season of new beginnings had come. This coffee shop was what kept me from crawling back into bed each day. It had to be perfect.

Our friends helped me put up shelves, and it gave us all a reason to continue to be together after she was gone. Telling stories in her memory and laughing at all the good times and crazy stories we never wanted to forget.

Lizzy was out front, digging up the dirt in front of the store, and Brad, David, and Maddy stood next to the apple tree. Victoria's mother told me she planted an apple tree when both Victoria and her sister were born and also when Lizzy was born. As they grew, so did the tree.

I decided a tree was exactly what I needed because it was a sign of life, and it reminded me of Victoria. Victoria's sister even volunteered to pick out a tree, and she made it here an hour before the grand opening. Just in time. And she was sober.

"It's time," Lyndsey said after she looked at her phone. "They're ready for us."

I grabbed the urn off the shelf and walked over to the dirt that was freshly shoveled.

"Today is the day Victoria and my dreams come true. We hoped we would be able to do this together, but God had another plan. She was taken from us too soon, but she will forever live on in all of our hearts and in the store."

Lizzy stepped forward, and I reached out and handed her the urn.

"Most of you know Victoria's dying wish was to be cremated and set free in the place she loved the most, here in Side Lake."

Lizzy sprinkled some ashes in the dirt and then handed the urn to Tim. I got down on my knees and Diane handed me the apple tree to plant. As the tears fell and my heart sank, I realized this was not the best idea for my grand opening.

Once I planted the tree and filled around it with dirt, my shoulders shook, and I lost total control of my emotions. Brad put his hand out and helped me to my feet. He pulled me in and patted my back as my whole body shook in his arms and my tears wet his shoulder.

I pulled myself together and wiped my eyes, my hands now on my hips. I looked away, then back at him. "How did you do it, man? How did you keep going when it hurt so bad you couldn't breathe?"

"I don't know, but you will get through this. You're doing everything the way you're supposed to. You're dealing with it and not numbing the pain another way."

Maddy stepped forward and squeezed my arm. "Victoria would want you to be happy. That's how Brad and I got through the hardest days. We're here by your side. You will never be alone."

As if on cue, Hope came running to my side and rubbed her head on my leg. She'd grown so much since Victoria passed away. She never got to see our fur baby get any bigger than a puppy.

Lizzy opened the door, and I led the way in as she flipped the sign and everyone cheered.

"I have something for you," Ethan said. He pulled me behind the counter and gave me a package with his PO Box on the front.

"What is this?"

"Just open it," he said.

Everyone else leaned on the bar and watched as I slid my key beneath the tape and opened up the heavy box. Inside was Ethan's newest book.

"It doesn't come out until next week, but I want you to have it in your store before anyone else."

I gave him a man hug with hard pats between his shoulders, then took out a book. "Madly in Love by Elizabeth Conrad."

Kat smiled. "Open it up and read the dedication."

I gave them both a curious look and opened it. "For Victoria and Troy Finney."

My eyes watered. I loved seeing her name still alive right next to mine. It was as if she was still with us. This book would live on far after we were all gone. Our names were forever tied together in a book that would soon be a New York Times bestseller like the rest.

"Thank you." I turned to Lizzy. "Would you please put these books in the window for me and post it on social media?"

"You got it." Tim grabbed the box and he and Lizzy organized the books in the front window and on an open shelf.

Kevin stood next to me and put his hand on my back. "Did Lizzy hear from the college about school yet?"

"She starts in the fall."

Lizzy tried to leave not too long after Victoria passed, but I offered her a job helping me around the house. The truth was, I wanted her with me. She was going to help me out with the store and around the house. She was great with Hope, and I knew it would not be long before Tim asked her to move in with him, so there was really no reason to make her get a place in Hibbing.

Tim brought home a ring last week and showed it to me. He said he knew she was the one, but I had to keep it a secret until he finally popped the question. I thought it would hurt more, seeing two people so in love, but what Victoria and I had was so strong I wanted everyone else I loved to know what it was like to feel the way we did.

No one would ever love anyone as much as I loved Victoria, but Lizzy and Tim were a close second.

As the boats pulled onto shore to visit my store, I smiled and looked at the giant picture of us displayed right above the door. Hope whimpered at my feet, and I bent down to pet her under the chin.

"Everything is going to be just fine, little girl. Your mama is right here with us, watching as her dreams are coming true. She wouldn't miss it for the world."

Acknowledgments

First off, I want to thank you, the reader for all your support throughout the years. Thank you for the reviews and recommending my books to your friends and family. There is no greater gift to an author. Thanks for falling in love with these characters as much as I have.

With a special thanks to the professionals that made this book possible: Shirley Fedorak, Kristin Bryant, April Krampotich, and all my proofreaders. It takes a village.

Thanks to the city of Side Lake and the Iron Range for all your love and support through the years. You guys are all amazing.

Thank you to my husband, Owen, for always being by my side at every book signing and listening to me go on and on about fictional characters and ideas when I get really into my books. Thank you for being my person and never complaining. You have such a big heart and I love you so much.

With thanks to my daughter, Alexis, for always reading my books and telling me when things just don't work. I love the way your creativity glows, never lose that. I know I can always go to you and know you will always be honest with me.

Lastly, thank you to my mother for making the magic of Christmas come alive in our house growing up, and still. For all those days making memories baking Christmas cookies with me and having the best decorations in town, inside and out. You always made sure to find a way to make it the best Christmas ever and blare Christmas music as we danced around the kitchen to Alabama, and it isn't Christmas without Dolly Parton and Kenny Rogers. I'm blessed to have been able to pass this tradition down to my children, and I know they will do the same with theirs. Thank you for teaching me the joy of Christmas, and the magic of the holidays. I love you.

If you enjoy my stories, please take a minute to write a quick and honest review online. It helps to get the word out to the world. Book five, the final book in the Turtle Creek Series, will be released Spring 2025. For more information please sign up for my email list and/or follow me on social media.

Facebook: @jenniferwaltersauthor
Instagram: @JenniferWaltersAuthor
TikTok: Jennifer Walters Author
Website: www.JenniferWaltersAuthor.com

Thank you for reading.

Printed in the USA
CPSIA information can be obtained
at www.ICGtesting.com
LVHW092337061224
798545LV00022B/568/J